PUF
RANJI'S WON
OTHER STORIES

Born in Kasauli in 1934, Ruskin Bond grew up in Jamnagar, Dehradun, New Delhi and Shimla. His first novel, *The Room on the Roof,* written when he was seventeen, received the John Llewellyn Rhys Memorial Prize in 1957. Since then he has written over five hundred short stories, essays and novellas (some included in the collections *Dust on the Mountains* and *Classic Ruskin Bond*) and more than forty books for children.

He received the Sahitya Akademi Award for English writing in India in 1993, the Padma Shri in 1999, and the Delhi government's Lifetime Achievement Award in 2012. He was awarded the Sahitya Akademi's Bal Sahitya Puraskar for his 'total contribution to children's literature' in 2013 and was honoured with the Padma Bhushan in 2014. He lives in Landour, Mussoorie, with his extended family.

Also in Puffin by Ruskin Bond

RUSKIN BOND

RANJI'S WONDERFUL BAT & OTHER STORIES

ILLUSTRATIONS BY

ARCHANA SREENIVASAN

PUFFIN BOOKS

PUFFIN BOOKS

Published by the Penguin Group

Penguin Books India Pvt. Ltd, 7th Floor, Infinity Tower C, DLF Cyber City, Gurgaon 122 002, Haryana, India

Penguin Group (USA) Inc., 375 Hudson Street, New York, New York 10014, USA

Penguin Group (Canada), 90 Eglinton Avenue East, Suite 700, Toronto, Ontario, M4P 2Y3, Canada

Penguin Books Ltd, 80 Strand, London WC2R 0RL, England

Penguin Ireland, 25 St Stephen's Green, Dublin 2, Ireland (a division of Penguin Books Ltd)

Penguin Group (Australia), 707 Collins Street, Melbourne, Victoria 3008, Australia

Penguin Group (NZ), 67 Apollo Drive, Rosedale, Auckland 0632, New Zealand

Penguin Books (South Africa) (Pty) Ltd, Block D, Rosebank Office Park, 181 Jan Smuts Avenue, Parktown North, Johannesburg 2193, South Africa

Penguin Books Ltd, Registered Offices: 80 Strand, London WC2R 0RL, England

First published in Puffin by Penguin Books India 2015

Copyright © Ruskin Bond 2015

Illustrations © Archana Sreenivasan 2015

All rights reserved

10 9 8 7 6 5 4 3 2 1

DISCLAIMER This is a work of fiction. Names, characters, places and incidents are either the product of the author's imagination or are used fictitiously and any resemblance to any actual person, living or dead, events or locales is entirely coincidental.

ISBN 9780143333128

Typeset in Cochin by Manipal Digital Systems
Printed at Replika Press Pvt. Ltd, India

This book is sold subject to the condition that it shall not, by way of trade or otherwise, be lent, resold, hired out, or otherwise circulated without the publisher's prior written consent in any form of binding or cover other than that in which it is published and without a similar condition including this condition being imposed on the subsequent purchaser and without limiting the rights under copyright reserved above, no part of this publication may be reproduced, stored in or introduced into a retrieval system, or transmitted in any form or by any means (electronic, mechanical, photocopying, recording or otherwise), without the prior written permission of both the copyright owner and the above-mentioned publisher of this book.

A PENGUIN RANDOM HOUSE COMPANY

Contents

Introduction

Back in the days when I played a little cricket, I wrote a few stories about the game—stories for children, featuring twelve-year-old Ranji, who appears in a number of my earlier stories.

In writing them, I wanted to bring out some of the joy and fun of playing or watching this great game. Over the years I have become somewhat disenchanted with it— match-fixing, controversies on and off the field, and other unpleasant features of the professional game. But I still like watching a group of schoolchildren, be they city kids or village children, enjoying the game in the winter sunshine, sometimes playing with borrowed bats or scuffed-up balls or wickets painted on walls.

'Ranji's Wonderful Bat' and 'Cricket for the Crocodile' were first published by Julia MacRae

Books in 1986 and 1988 respectively, as well as in a couple of school readers. As this is a collection of stories about sporting activities in general, I have included a couple of my 'Uncle Ken' stories; also an account of a tremendous bicycle ride through a forest fire; a beetle race; a Boy Scouts' Camp; and a trek to a Himalayan glacier. This last was based on a trek I made to the Pindari Glacier, in Kumaon, with a group of student friends.

All celebrations of childhood, boyhood, girlhood (don't forget Koki), youth and the spirit of adventure. The great outdoors still beckons, for those who can drag themselves away from their laptops!

Ruskin Bond
Winter of 2014-15

Ranji's Wonderful Bat

'How's that!' shouted the wicketkeeper, holding the ball up in his gloves.

'How's that!' echoed the slip fielders.

'How?' growled the fast bowler, glaring at the umpire.

'Out!' said the umpire.

And Suraj, the captain of the school team, was walking slowly back to the Pavilion — which was really a tool shed at the end of the field.

The score stood at 53 for 4 wickets. Another 60 runs had to be made for victory, and only one good batsman remained. All the rest were bowlers who couldn't be expected to make many runs.

It was Ranji's turn to bat.

He was the youngest member of the team, only eleven, but sturdy and full of pluck. As he walked briskly to the wicket, his unruly black hair was blown about by a cool breeze that came down from the hills.

Ranji had a good eye and strong wrists, and had made lots of runs in some of the minor matches. But in the last two inter school games, his scores had been poor, the highest being 12 runs. Now he was determined to make enough runs to take his side to victory.

Ranji took his guard and prepared to face the bowler. The fielders moved closer, in anticipation of another catch. The tall fast bowler scowled and began his long run. His arm whirled over, and the hard shiny red ball came hurtling towards Ranji.

Ranji was going to lunge forward and play the ball back to the bowler, but at the last moment he changed his mind and stepped back, intending to push the ball through the ring of fielders on his right or offside.

'How's that!' screamed the bowler hopping about like a kangaroo.

'How?' shouted the wicketkeeper.

The umpire slowly raised a finger.

'Out,' he said.

'Never mind,' said Suraj, patting Ranji on the back.
'You'll do better next time. You're out of form just now,
that's all.'

'You'll have to make more runs in the next game,'
he told Ranji, 'or you'll lose your place in the side!'

Avoiding the other players, Ranji walked slowly
homewards, his head down, his hands in his pockets.
He was very upset. He had been trying so hard and
practising so regularly, but when an important game
came along he failed to make a big score. It seemed
that there was nothing he could do about it. But he
loved playing cricket, and he couldn't bear the thought
of being out of the school team.

On his way home he had to pass the clock tower,
where he often stopped at Mr Kumar's Sports Shop,
to chat with the owner or look at all the things on the
shelves: footballs, cricket balls, badminton rackets,
hockey sticks, balls of various shapes and sizes—it
was a wonderland where Ranji liked to linger every
day.

But this was one day when he didn't feel like
stopping. He looked the other way and was about to
cross the road when Mr Kumar's voice stopped him.

'Hello, Ranji! Off in a hurry today? And why are
you looking so sad?'

So Ranji had to stop and say namaste. He couldn't ignore Mr Kumar, who had always been so kind and helpful, often giving him advice on how to play different kinds of bowling. Mr Kumar had been a state player once, and had scored a century in a match against Tanzania. Now he liked encouraging young players and he thought Ranji would make a good cricketer.

'What's the trouble?' he asked as Ranji stepped into the shop. Because Mr Kumar was so friendly, the sports goods also seemed friendly. The bats and balls and shuttlecocks all seemed to want to be helpful.

'We lost the match,' said Ranji.

'Never mind,' said Mr Kumar. 'Where would we be without losers? There wouldn't be any games without them — no cricket or football or hockey or tennis! No carom or marbles. No sports shop for me! Anyway, how many runs did you make?'

'None, I made a big round egg.'

Mr Kumar rested his hand on Ranji's shoulder. 'Never mind. All good players have a bad day now and then.'

'But I haven't made a good score in my last three matches,' said Ranji. 'I'll be dropped from the team if I don't do something in the next game.'

'Well, we can't have that happening,' mused Mr Kumar. 'Something will have to be done about it.'

'I'm just unlucky,' said Ranji.

'Maybe, maybe . . . but in that case, it's time your luck changed.'

'It's too late now,' said Ranji.

'Nonsense. It's never too late. Now, you just come with me to the back of the shop and I'll see if I can do something about your luck.'

Puzzled, Ranji followed Mr Kumar through the curtained partition at the back of the shop. He found himself in a badly-lit room stacked to the ceiling with all kinds of old and second-hand sporting goods—torn football bladders, broken bats, rackets without strings, broken darts, and tattered badminton nets.

Mr Kumar began examining a number of old cricket bats, and after a few minutes he said, 'Ah!' Picking up one of the bats he held it out to Ranji.

'This is it!' he said. 'This is the luckiest of all my old bats. This is the bat I made a century with!' He gave it a twirl and started hitting an imaginary ball to all corners of the room.

'Of course it's an old bat, but it hasn't lost any of its magic,' said Mr Kumar, pausing in his stroke-making to recover his breath. He held it out to Ranji. 'Here, take it!' I'll lend it to you for the rest of the cricket season. You won't fail with it.'

Ranji took the bat and gazed at it with awe and delight.

'Is it really the bat you made a century with?' he asked.

'It is,' said Mr Kumar. 'And it may get you a hundred runs too!'

Ranji spent a nervous week waiting for Saturday's match. His school team would be playing a strong side from another town. There was a lot of classwork that week, so Ranji did not get much time to practise with the other boys. As he had no brothers or sisters he asked Koki, the girl next door, to bowl to him in the garden. Koki bowled quite well, but Ranji liked to hit the ball hard—'just to get used to the bat,' he told her—and she soon got tired of chasing the ball all over the garden.

At last Saturday arrived, bright and sunny and just right for cricket.

Suraj won the toss for the school and took batting first.

The opening batsman put on 30 runs without being separated. The visiting fast bowlers couldn't do much. Then the spin bowlers came on, and immediately there was a change in the game. Two wickets fell in one over, and the score was 33 for 2. Suraj made a few quick runs, then he too was out to one of the spinners, caught behind the wicket. The next batsman was clean bowled — 46 for 4 — and it was Ranji's turn to bat.

He walked slowly to the wicket. The fielders crowded round him. He took guard and prepared for the first ball.

The bowler took a short run and then the ball was twirling towards Ranji, looking as though it would spin away from his bat as he leaned forward into his stroke.

And then a thrill ran through Ranji's arm as he felt the ball meet the springy willow of the bat.

Crack!

The ball, hit firmly with the middle of Ranji's bat, streaked past the helpless bowler and sped towards the boundary. Four runs!

The bowler was annoyed, with the result that his next ball was a loose full toss. Ranji swung it to the onside boundary for another four.

And that was only the beginning. Now Ranji began to play all the strokes he knew: late cuts and square cuts, straight drives, on drives and off drives. The rival captain tried all his bowlers, fast and spin, but none of them could remove Ranji. Instead he sent the fielders scampering to all corners of the field.

By the lunch break he had scored 40. And twenty minutes after lunch, when Suraj closed the innings, Ranji was not out with 58.

The rival team was bowled out for a poor score, and Ranji's school won the match.

On his way home Ranji stopped at Mr Kumar's shop to give him the good news.

'We won!' he said. 'And I made 58—my highest score so far. It really is a lucky bat!'

'I told you so,' said Mr Kumar, giving Ranji a warm handshake. 'There'll be bigger scores yet.'

Ranji went home in high spirits. He was so pleased that he stopped at the Jumma Sweet Shop and bought two laddus for Koki. She was crazy about laddu.

Mr Kumar was right. It was only the beginning of Ranji's success with the bat. In the next game he scored 40, and was out when he grew careless and allowed himself to be stumped by the wicketkeeper. The game that followed was a two-day match, and Ranji, who was now batting at Number 3, made 45 runs. He hit a number of boundaries before being caught. In the second innings, when the school team needed only 6 runs for victory, Ranji was batting at 25 when the winning runs were hit.

Everyone was pleased with him—his coach, his captain, Suraj and Mr Kumar—but no one knew about the lucky bat. That was a secret between Ranji and Mr Kumar.

One evening, during an informal game on the maidan, Ranji's friend Bhim slipped while running after the ball, and cut his hand on a sharp stone. Ranji took him to a doctor near the clock tower, where the wound was washed and bandaged. As it was getting late, he decided to go straight home. Usually he walked, but that evening he caught a bus near the clock tower.

When he got home, his mother brought him a cup of tea, and while he was drinking it, Koki walked in, and the first thing she said was, 'Ranji, where's your bat?'

'Oh, I must have left it on the maidan when Bhim got hurt,' said Ranji, starting up and spilling his tea. 'I'd better go and get it now, or it will disappear.'

'You can fetch it tomorrow,' said his mother. 'It's getting dark.'

'I'll take a torch,' said Ranji.

He was worried about the bat.

Without it, his luck might desert him.

He hadn't the patience to wait for a bus, and ran all the way to the maidan.

The maidan was deserted, and there was no sign of the bat. And then Ranji remembered that he'd had it with him on the bus, after saying goodbye to Bhim at the clock tower. He must have left it on the bus!

Well, he'd never find it now. The bat was lost forever. And on Saturday Ranji's school would be playing their last and most important match of the cricket season against a public school team from Delhi.

Next day he was at Mr Kumar's shop, looking very sorry for himself.

'What's the matter?' asked Mr Kumar.

'I've lost the bat,' said Ranji. 'Your lucky bat. The one I made all my runs with! I left it in the bus. And the day after tomorrow we are playing the Delhi school, and I'll be out for a duck, and we'll lose our chance of being the school champions.'

Mr Kumar looked a little anxious at first; then he smiled and said, 'You can still make all the runs you want.'

'But I don't have the bat any more,' said Ranji.

'Any bat will do,' said Mr Kumar.

'What do you mean?'

'I mean it's the batsman and not the bat that matters. Shall I tell you something? That old bat I gave you was no different from any other bat I've used. True, I made a lot of runs with it, but I made runs with other bats too. A bat has magic only when the batsman has magic! What you needed was confidence, not a bat. And by believing in the bat, you got your confidence back!'

'What's confidence?' asked Ranji. It was a new word for him.

'Con-fi-dence,' said Mr Kumar slowly. 'Confidence is knowing you are good.'

'And I can be good without the bat?'

'Of course. You have always been good. You are good now. You will be good the day after tomorrow. Remember that. If you remember it, you'll make the runs.'

On Saturday Ranji walked to the wicket with a bat borrowed from Bhim.

The school team had lost its first wicket with only 2 runs on the board. Ranji went in at this stage. The Delhi school's opening bowler was sending down some really fast ones. Ranji faced up to him.

The first ball was very fast but it wasn't on a good length. Quick on his feet, Ranji stepped back and pulled it hard to the onside boundary. The ball soared over the heads of the fielders and landed with a crash in a crate full of cold drink bottles.

A six! Everyone stood up and cheered.

And it was only the beginning of Ranji's wonderful innings.

The match ended in a draw, but Ranji's 75 was the talk of the school.

On his way home he bought a dozen laddus. Six for Koki and six for Mr Kumar.

Koki Plays the Game

'There's a cricket match on Saturday, isn't there?' asked Koki.

'That's right,' replied Ranji. 'We're playing the Public School team.'

'I might come and watch,' said Koki.

'As you like. It won't be much of a game. We'll beat them easily.'

Ranji's own cricket team was quite different from his school team. It consisted of boys, big and small, long and short, from various walks of life. Even Koki, a girl, was allowed honorary membership, and had sometimes been 'twelfth man'—an extra; but she knew the game well, and often bowled to Ranji in the mornings, when he wanted batting practice. Only a couple of team members could afford to go to private schools like Ranji; most of them went to the local government school, and two or three had stopped going to school altogether.

There was Bhartu, who delivered newspapers in the mornings; and the brothers Mukesh and Rakesh, whose father had a sweet shop; and a tailor's son, Amir Ali; and Billy Jones, an Anglo-Indian; and 'Lumboo'— the Tall one; and Sitaram, the washerman's son, and several others. And there was also Amar who couldn't play at all, but who made a good umpire (when his glasses weren't steamed over) and who accompanied the team wherever it went.

This Saturday they were playing on their 'home' ground, a patch of wasteland behind a new cinema hall called Apsara.

The Public School boys had arrived first, which was only natural since they all lived in the same boarding school. The members of Ranji's team came from different directions, so it was some time before they had all assembled. Even then they were two short. But Ranji won the toss and decided to bat, hoping that the missing team members would arrive in time to take their turn at the wicket.

'If Mukesh and Rakesh aren't here in time, we won't have them in the team,' said Ranji sternly.

'Don't sack them,' said Lumboo. 'They always bring us sweets and snacks from their father's shop. We need them in the team even if they don't score any runs.'

'Well if they turn up without refreshments, they'll be sacked,' said Ranji, always ready to be fair.

The two umpires had gone out to set up the stumps — Amar, on behalf of Ranji's team, and a teacher from the Public School.

'I don't like the look of that teacher,' said Amir Ali.

'Well, we won't take any risks.'

Billy Jones and Lumboo always opened batting. Lumboo's height helped him to deal with the fast rising ball. He took the first ball.

The Public School's opening bowler was speedy but inaccurate. This was because he was trying to bowl too fast. His first ball went for a wide, but it was still about a foot from the leg stump. Lumboo took a swipe at it and missed. The third ball pitched halfway down the wicket and kept low. It struck Lumboo on the pads.

'How's that!' shouted the bowler, wicketkeeper and slip fielders in unison.

The Public School's umpire did not hesitate. Up went his finger. Lumboo was given out leg before wicket.

Lumboo stood aghast. He looked down at where his feet were placed, then back at his stumps.

'I'm not in front of the wicket,' he complained, to no one in particular.

'The umpire's word is law,' said the wicketkeeper.

Lumboo walked slowly back to where his teammates reclined against a pile of bricks.

'I wasn't out!' he protested.

'Never mind,' said Ranji, whose turn it was to bat. 'You'll get your chance when you come on to bowl.'

He walked to the wicket with a confident air, his bat resting on his shoulder. He took guard carefully and, tapping his bat on the ground, faced the bowler. It sped to the boundary, amidst delighted cries from Ranji's teammates. Four runs.

The next ball was short, just outside the off stump. Ranji stepped back and square cut it past point. Another four. There were more cheers, and this time Ranji distinctly heard a girl's voice, shouting, 'Good shot, Ranji!'

He looked back to where his team members were gathered. There was no girl among them. He turned and looked towards the opposite boundary, and there, under the giant cinema hoarding, stood Koki. She waved to him.

Settling down to face the bowler again, Ranji was aware of two things at once—of the bowler making faces and charging up to bowl, and of Koki standing on the boundary and waiting for him to hit another four. This loss in concentration caused him to misjudge the next ball. Instead of playing forward, he played back. The ball took the edge of his bat and flew straight into the wicketkeeper's gloves.

'How's that!' shouted all the fielders appealing for a catch.

Ranji did not wait for the umpire—in this case, Amar—to give him out. He knew he'd touched the ball. Scowling, he walked back to his team. It was all Koki's fault!

Now there was a good partnership between Sitaram and Bhartu. Sitaram, who helped his father with the town's washing on Sundays, was in the habit of laying out clothes on a flat stone and pounding them with a stout stick—the method followed by most washermen. He dealt with the cricket ball in much the same way— clouting it hard, and sending it to various points of the compass. He hit up 25 valuable runs before he was out, caught off a big hit. Bhartu pushed and prodded, merely keeping one end going, until he too was out to an lbw decision. Billy Jones had gone the same way, taking the ball on his pads. No one was happy with the lbw decisions.

'We must have neutral umpires,' said Amir Ali.

'But who wants to be an umpire?' asked Ranji. 'We won't have anyone. We'll have to use our team members—or let the other side provide *both* umpires!'

'Not after today,' said Lumboo.

Meanwhile, Mukesh and Rakesh had arrived, carrying paper bags full of samosas and jalebis. As a result, everyone cheered up. Wickets fell almost as rapidly as the snacks and sweets were consumed. Mukesh and Rakesh, who were the last men in, held out for several overs until Rakesh was given out lbw. Ranji's team was all out for 87 runs—not really a match-winning score, except on a tricky wicket.

It was the Public School team's turn to bat. One of their opening batsmen was bowled by Lumboo for nought. The other batsman was twice rapped on the pads by balls from Ranji, but his loud appeals for lbw were turned down—by the Public School umpire, naturally! Muttering to himself, Ranji hurled down a thunderbolt of a ball. It rose sharply and struck the batsman on the hand. Howling with pain, he dropped his bat and wrung his hand. Then he showed everyone a swollen finger and decided to 'retire hurt'.

'There's more than one way of getting them out,' muttered Ranji as he passed the umpire.

The next two batsmen were good players, not as nervous as the openers. One of them got what might have been a faint tickle to an outswinger from Lumboo, but he was given the benefit of the doubt by Amar who, as umpires went, was as impartial as a star. He showed no favours to his own team, no matter what the other umpire did. It just isn't fair, thought Ranji . . .

The number three and four batsmen put on 40 runs between them, and by mid-afternoon Ranji's players were feeling tired and hungry. Then three quick wickets fell to Sitaram's spinners. Three wickets remained, and 20 runs were needed for the Public School victory.

This was when Bhartu, running to take a catch, collided with chubby Mukesh. Both of them went sprawling on the grass, and when they got up, the ball was found lodged in the back of Mukesh's pants. How it got there no one could tell, but after much discussion the umpires had to agree that it qualified as a catch and the batsman was given out. But Bhartu had to leave the ground with a bleeding nose.

Ranji looked around for a replacement. There was no one in sight except Koki.

'Come and field,' said Ranji brusquely.

Koki needed no persuading. She slipped off her sandals and dashed barefoot on to the field, taking up Bhartu's position near the boundary.

The tail-end batsmen were now swinging at the ball in a desperate attempt to hit off the remaining runs. A hard-hit drive sped past Koki and went for 4 runs. Ranji gave her a hard look. Then the two batsmen got into a muddle while trying to take a quick run, and one of them was run out.

The last man came in. The Public School was 8 runs behind, but a couple of boundaries would take care of that.

The batsmen took two runs. And then, one of them, overconfident and sure of victory, swung out at a slow, tempting ball from Sitaram, and the ball flew towards Koki in a long, curving arc.

Koki had to run a few yards to her left. Then she leapt like a gazelle and took the ball in both hands.

Ranji's team had won, and Koki had made the winning catch.

It was her last appearance as 'twelfth man'. From that day onwards Koki was a regular member of the team.

Cricket for the Crocodile

I

Ranji was up at dawn. It was Sunday, a school holiday. Although he was supposed to be preparing for his exams, only a fortnight away, he couldn't resist one or two more games before getting down to history and algebra and other unexciting things.

'I'm going to be a Test cricketer when I grow up,' he told his mother. 'Of what use will maths be to me?' 'You never know,' said his mother, who happened to be more of a cricket fan than his father. 'You might need maths to work out your batting average. And as for history, wouldn't you like to be a part of history? Famous cricketers make history!'

'Making history is all right,' said Ranji. 'As long as I don't have to remember the date on which I make it!'

Ranji met his friends and teammates in the park. The grass was still wet with dew, the sun only just rising behind the distant hills. The park was full of flower beds, and swings and slides for smaller children. The boys would have to play on the riverbank against their rivals, the village boys. Ranji did not have a full team that morning, but he was just looking for a friendly match. The really important game would be held the following Sunday.

The village team was quite good because the boys lived near each other and practised a lot together, whereas Ranji's team was drawn from all parts of the town. There was the baker's boy, Nathu; the tailor's son, Sunder; the postmaster's son, Prem; and the bank manager's son, Anil. These were some of the better players. Sometimes their fathers also turned up for a game. The fathers weren't very good, but you couldn't tell them that. After all, they helped to provide bats and balls and pocket money.

A regular spectator at these matches was Nakoo the crocodile, who lived in the river. Nakoo means Nosey, but the village boys were very respectful and called him Nakoo-ji. He had a long snout, rows of ugly-looking teeth (some of them badly in need of fillings), and a powerful scaly tail.

He was nearly fifteen feet long, but you did not see much of him; he swam low in the water and glided smoothly through the tall grasses near the riverbank to bask in the sun. He did not care for people, especially cricketers. He disliked the noise they made, frightening away the waterbirds and other creatures required for an interesting menu, and it was also alarming to have cricket balls plopping around in the shallows where he liked to rest.

Once Nakoo crept quite close to the bank manager, who was resting against one of the trees near the riverbank. The bank manager was a portly gentleman, and Nakoo seemed to think he would make a good meal. Just then a party of villagers had come along, beating drums for a wedding procession. Nakoo retired to the muddy waters of the river. He was a little tired of swallowing frogs, eels and herons. That juicy bank manager would make a nice change—he'd grab him one day.

II

The village boys were a little older than Ranji and his friends, but they did not bring their fathers along. The game made very little sense to the older villagers. And when balls came flying across fields to land in milk pails or cooking pots, they were as annoyed as the crocodile.

Today, the men were busy in the fields, and Nakoo the crocodile was wallowing in the mud behind a screen of reeds and water lilies. How beautiful and innocent those lilies looked! Only sharp eyes would have noticed Nakoo's long snout thrusting above the broad flat leaves of the lilies. His eyes were slits. He was watching.

Ranji struck the ball hard and high. Splash! It fell into the river about thirty feet from where Nakoo lay. Village boys and town boys dashed into the shallow water to look for the ball. Too many of them! Crowds made Nakoo nervous. He slid away, crossed the river to the opposite bank, and sulked.

As it was a warm day, nobody seemed to want to get out of the water. Several boys threw off their clothes, deciding that it was a better day for swimming than for cricket. Nakoo's mouth watered as he watched those bare limbs splashing about.

'We're supposed to be practising,' said Ranji, who took his cricket seriously. 'We won't win next week.'

'Oh, we'll win easily,' said Anil, joining him on the riverbank. 'My father says he's going to play.'

'The last time he played, we lost,' said Ranji. 'He made two runs and forgot to field.'

'He was out of form,' said Anil, ever loyal to his father, the bank manager.

Sheroo, the captain of the village team, joined them. 'My cousin from Delhi is going to play for us. He made a hundred in one of the matches there.'

'He won't make a hundred on this wicket,' said Ranji. 'It's slow at one end and fast at the other.'

'Can I bring my father?' asked Nathu, the baker's son.

'Can he play?'

'Not too well, but he'll bring along a basket of biscuits, buns and pakoras.'

'Then he can play,' said Ranji, always quick to make up his mind. No wonder he was the team's captain! 'If there are too many of us, we'll make him twelfth man.'

The ball could not be found and, as they did not want to risk their spare ball, the practice session was declared over.

'My grandfather's promised me a new ball,' said little Mani, from the village team, who bowled tricky leg breaks which bounced to the offside.

'Does he want to play, too?' asked Ranji.

'No, of course not. He's nearly eighty.'

'That's settled then,' said Ranji. 'We'll all meet here at nine o'clock next Sunday. Fifty overs a side.'

They broke up, Sheroo and his team wandering back to the village, while Ranji and his friends got on to their bicycles (two or three to a bicycle, since not everyone had one), and cycled back to town.

Nakoo, left in peace at last, returned to his favourite side of the river and crawled some way up the river bank, as if to inspect the wicket. It had been worn smooth by the players, and looked like a good place to relax. Nakoo moved across it. He felt pleasantly drowsy in the warm sun, so he closed his eyes for a little nap. It was good to be out of the water for a while.

III

The following Sunday morning, a cycle bell tinkled at the gate. It was Nathu, waiting for Ranji to join him. Ranji hurried out of the house, carrying his bat and a thermos of lime juice thoughtfully provided by his mother.

'Have you got the stumps?' he asked.

'Sunder has them.'

'And the ball?'

'Yes. And Anil's father is bringing one too, provided he opens the batting!'

Nathu rode, while Ranji sat on the crossbar with bat and thermos. Anil was waiting for them outside his house.

'My father's gone ahead on his scooter. He's picking up Nathu's father. Follow with Prem and Sunder.'

Most of the boys got to the riverbank before the bank manager and the baker. They left their bicycles under a shady banyan tree and ran down the gentle slope to the river. And then, one by one they stopped, astonished by what they saw.

They gaped in awe at their cricket pitch.

Across it, basking in the soft warm sunshine, was Nakoo the crocodile.

'Where did it come from ?' asked Ranji.

'Usually he stays in the river,' said Sheroo, who had joined them. 'But all this week he's been coming out to lie on our wicket. I don't think he wants us to play.'

'We'll have to get him off,' said Ranji.

'You'd better keep out of reach of his tail and jaws!'

'We'll wait until he goes away,' said Prem.

But Nakoo showed no signs of wanting to leave. He rather liked the smooth flat stretch of ground which he had discovered. And now here were all those boys again, doing their best to disturb him.

After some time the boys began throwing pebbles at Nakoo. These had no effect, simply bouncing off the crocodile's thick hide. They tried mud balls and an orange. Nakoo twitched his tail and opened one eye, but refused to move on.

Then Prem took a ball, and bowled a fast one at the crocodile. It bounced just short of Nakoo and caught him on the snout. Startled and stung, he wriggled off the pitch and moved rapidly down the riverbank and into the water. There was a mighty splash as he dived for cover.

'Well bowled, Prem!' said Ranji. 'That was a good ball.'

'Nakoo-ji will be in a bad mood after that,' warned Sheroo. 'Don't get too close to the river.'

The bank manager and the baker were the last to arrive. The scooter had given them some trouble. No one mentioned the crocodile, just in case the adults decided to call the match off.

After inspecting the wicket, which Nakoo had left in fair condition, Sheroo and Ranji tossed a coin. Ranji called 'Heads!' but it came up tails. Sheroo chose to bat first.

IV

The tall Delhi player came out to open the innings with little Mani.

Mani was a steady bat, who could stay at the wicket for a long time, but in a one-day match, quick scoring was needed. This the Delhi player provided. He struck a four, then took a single off the last ball of the over. It gave him the strike and he took 8 runs off the next over.

In the third over, Mani tried to hit out and was bowled for a duck. So the village team's score was 13 for 1.

'Well done,' said Ranji to fast bowler Prem. 'But we'll have to get that tall fellow out soon. He seems quite good.' The tall fellow showed no sign of getting out. He hit two more boundaries and then swung one hard and high towards the river.

Nakoo, who had been sulking in the shallows, saw the ball coming towards him. He opened his jaws wide and, with a satisfying 'clunk', the ball lodged between his back teeth.

Nakoo got his teeth deep into the cricket ball and chewed. Revenge was sweet. And the ball tasted good, too. The combination of leather and cork was just right. Nakoo decided that he would snap up any other balls that came his way.

'Harmless old reptile,' said the bank manager. He produced a new ball and insisted that he bowl with it.

It proved to be the most expensive over of the match. The bank manager's bowling was quite harmless and the Delhi player kept hitting the ball into the fields for fours and sixes. The score soon mounted to 40 for 1. The bank manager modestly took himself off.

By the time the tenth over had been bowled, the score had mounted to 70. Then Ranji, bowling slow spins, lost his grip on the ball and sent the batsman a full toss. Having played the good balls perfectly, the Delhi player couldn't resist taking a mighty swipe at the bad ball. He mistimed his shot, and was astonished to see the ball fall into the hands of a fielder near the boundary. Seventy for 2. The game was far from being lost for Ranji's team.

A couple of wickets fell cheaply, and then Sheroo came in and started playing rather well. His drives were straight and clean. The ball cut down the buttercups and hummed over the grass. A big hit landed in a poultry yard. Feathers flew and so did curses. Nakoo raised his head to see what all the noise was about. No further cricket balls came his way, and he gazed balefully at a heron who was staying just out of his reach.

The score mounted steadily. The fielding grew slack, as it often does when batsmen gain the upper hand. A catch was dropped. And Nathu's father, keeping wicket, missed a stumping chance.

'No more grown-ups in our team,' grumbled Nathu. The baker made amends by taking a good catch behind the wicket. The score was 115 for 5, with about half the overs remaining.

Sheroo kept his end up, but the other batsmen struggled for runs and the end came with about 5 overs still to go. A modest total of 145.

'Should be easy,' said Ranji.

'No problem,' said Prem.

'Lunch first,' said the bank manager, and they took a half-hour break.

The village boys went to their homes for rest and refreshment, while Ranji and his team spread themselves out under the banyan tree.

Nathu's father had brought patties and pakoras; the bank manager had brought a basket of oranges and bananas; Prem had brought jackfruit curry; Ranji had brought carrot halwa; Sunder had brought a large container full of peas pulao; and the others had brought various curries, pickles and sauces. Everything was shared, and with the picnic in full swing no one noticed that Nakoo the crocodile had left the water. Using some tall reeds as cover, he had crept halfway up the riverbank. Those delicious food smells had reached him too, and he was unwilling to be left out of the picnic. Perhaps the boys would leave something for him. If not . . .

'Time to start,' announced the bank manager, getting up. 'I'll open the batting. We need a good start if we are going to win.'

V

The bank manager strode out to the wicket in the company of young Nathu; Sheroo opened the bowling for the village team.

The bank manager took a run off the first ball. He puffed himself up and waved his bat in the air as though the match had already been won. Nathu played out the rest of the over without taking any chances.

The tall Delhi player took up the bowling from the other end. The bank manager tapped his bat impatiently, then raised it above his shoulders, ready to hit out. The bowler took a long, fast run up to the bowling crease. He gave a little leap, his arm swung over, and the ball came at the bank manager in a swift, curving flight.

The bank manager still had his bat raised when the ball flew past him and uprooted his middle stump.

A shout of joy went up from back to the fielders. The bank manager was on his way back to the shade of the banyan tree.

'A fly got in my eye,' he muttered. 'I wasn't ready. Flies everywhere!' And he swatted angrily at flies that no one else could see.

The villagers, hearing that someone as important as a bank manager was in their midst, decided that it would be wrong for him to sit on the ground like everyone else. So they brought him a cot from the village. It was one of those light wooden beds, taped with strands of thin rope. The bank manager lowered himself into it rather gingerly. It creaked but took his weight.

The score was 1 for 1. Anil took his father's place at the wicket and scored ten runs in two overs. The bank manager pretended not to notice but he was really quite pleased. 'Takes after me,' he said, and made himself comfortable on the cot.

Nathu kept his end up while Anil scored the runs. Then Anil was out, skying a catch to mid-wicket.

Twenty-five for 2 in six overs. It could have been worse.

'Well played!' called the bank manager to his son, and then lost interest in the proceedings. He was soon fast asleep on the cot. The flies did not seem to bother him any more.

Nathu kept going, and there were a couple of good partnerships for the fourth and fifth wickets. When the Delhi player finished his share of overs, the batsmen became freer in their strokeplay. Then little Mani got a ball to spin sharply, and Nathu was caught by the wicketkeeper.

It was 75 for 4 when Ranji came in to bat.

Before he could score a run, his partner at the other end was bowled. And then Nathu's father strode up to the wicket, determined to do better than the bank manager. In this he succeeded — by one run.

The baker scored two, and then, in trying to run another two when there was only one to be had, found himself stranded halfway up the wicket. The wicketkeeper knocked his stumps down.

The boys were too polite to say anything. And as for the bank manager he was now fast asleep under the banyan tree.

So intent was everyone on watching the match that no one noticed that Nakoo the crocodile had crept further up the riverbank to slide beneath the cot on which the bank manager was sleeping.

There was just room enough for Nakoo to get between the legs of the cot. He thought it was a good place to lie concealed, and he seemed not to notice the large man sleeping peacefully just above him.

Soon the bank manager was snoring gently, and it was not long before Nakoo dozed off, too. Only, instead of snoring, Nakoo appeared to be whistling, through his crooked teeth.

VI

Seventy-five for 5 and it looked as though Ranji's team would soon be crashing to defeat.

Sunder joined Ranji and, to everyone's delight, played two lovely drives to the boundary. Then Ranji got into his stride and cut and drove the ball for successive fours. The score began to mount steadily—112 for 5. Once again there were visions of victory.

After Sunder was out, stumped, Ranji was joined by Prem, a big hitter. Runs came quickly. The score reached 140. Only 6 runs were needed for victory.

Ranji decided to do it in style. Receiving a half-volley, he drove the ball hard and high towards the banyan tree.

Thump! It struck Nakoo on the jaw and loosened one of his teeth.

It was the second time that day he'd been caught napping. He'd had enough of it.

Nakoo lunged forward, tail thrashing and jaws snapping. The cot, with the manager still on it, rose with him. Crocodile and cot were now jammed together, and when Nakoo rushed forward, he took the cot with him.

The bank manager, dreaming that he was at sea in a rowing boat, woke up to find the cot pitching violently from side to side.

'Help!' he shouted. 'Help!'

The boys scattered in all directions, for the crocodile was now advancing down the wicket, knocking over stumps and digging up the pitch. He found an abandoned sun hat and swallowed it. A wicketkeeper's glove went the same way. A batsman's pad was caught up on his tail.

All this time the bank manager hung on to the cot for dear life, as it rocked and plunged about with the crocodile's heavings. He wondered if he should try and jump to safety, but would he be able to get out of reach of Nakoo's jaws and tail? He decided to hang on to the cot until it was dislodged.

'Come on, boys, help!' he shouted. 'Get me off!'

But the cot remained firmly attached to the crocodile, and so did the bank manager.

The problem was solved when Nakoo made for the river and plunged into its familiar waters. Then the bank manager tumbled into the water and scrambled up the riverbank, while Nakoo made for the opposite shore.

The bank manager's ordeal was over, and so was the cricket match.

'Did you see how I dealt with that crocodile?' he said, still dripping, but in better humour now that he was safe again. 'By the way, who won the match?'

'We don't know,' said Ranji, as they trudged back to their bicycles. 'That would have been a six if you hadn't been in the way.'

Sheroo, who had accompanied them as far as the main road, offered a return match the following week.

'I'm busy next week,' said the baker.

'I have another game,' said the bank manager.

'What game is that, sir?' asked Ranji.

'Chess,' replied the bank manager.

Ranji and his friends began making plans for the next match.

'You won't win without us,' said the bank manager.

'Not a chance,' said the baker.

But Ranji's team did, in fact, win that next match.

Nakoo the crocodile did not trouble them, because the cot was still attached to his back, and it took him several weeks to get it off.

A number of people came to the riverbank to look at the crocodile who carried his own bed around.

Some even stayed to watch the cricket.

George and Ranji

When I heard that my cousin George had again escaped from the mental hospital in a neighbouring town, I knew it wouldn't be long before he turned up at my doorstep. It usually happens at the approach of the cricket season. No problem, I thought. I'll just bundle him into a train and take him back to the hospital.

Cousin George had been there, off and on, for a few years. He wasn't the violent type and was given a certain amount of freedom, with the result that he occasionally wandered off by himself, sometimes to try and take in a Test match. You see, George did not suffer from the delusion that he was Napoleon or Ghengis Khan, he was convinced that he was selected to captain

India—quite forgetting that the great Ranjit Singhji had actually played for England!

So when George turned up on my front step I wasn't surprised to find him carrying a cricket bat in one hand and a protective box in the other.

'Aren't you ready?' he asked. 'The match starts at eleven'.

'There's plenty of time,' I said, recalling that the train left at eleven-fifteen. 'Why don't you come in and relax while I get ready?'

George sat down and asked for a glass of beer. I brought him one and he promptly emptied it over a pot of ferns.

'They look thirsty,' he said. I dressed hurriedly, anxious to get moving before he started his latest cuts on my cut glass decanter. Then, arm-in-arm, we walked to the gate and hailed an auto rickshaw.

'Railway station,' I whispered to the driver.

'Ferozshah Kotla,' said George in rising tones, naming Delhi's famous cricket ground. No matter, I thought, I'll straighten out the driver as we go along. I bundled George into the rickshaw and we were soon heading in the direction of Kotla.

'Railway station,' I said again, in tones that could not be denied.

'Kotla,' said cousin George, just as firmly.

The scooter driver kept right on course for the cricket ground. Apparently George had made a better impression on him.

'Look,' I said, tapping the driver on the shoulder. 'This is my cousin and he's not quite right in the head. He's just escaped from the mental asylum and if I'm to get him back there tonight, we must catch the eleven-fifteen train.'

The scooter driver slowed down and looked from Cousin George to me and back again. George gave him a winning smile and looking in my direction, tapped his forehead significantly. The driver nodded in sympathy and kept straight on for the stadium.

Well, I've always believed that the dividing line between sanity and insanity is a very thin one, but I had never realized it was quite so thin—too thin for my own comfort! Who was crazy, George, me or the driver?

We had almost reached Kotla and I had no intention of watching over Cousin George through a whole day's play. He gets excited at cricket matches—which is strange considering how strange they can be. On one occasion, he broke through the barriers and walked up to the wicket with his bat, determined to bat at Number 3 (Ranji's favourite position, apparently) and assaulted an umpire who tried to escort him from the ground. On another occasion he streaked across the ground, wearing nothing but his protective box.

But it was I who confirmed the driver's worst fears by jumping off the rickshaw as it slowed, and making my getaway. I've never been able to discover if Cousin George had any money with him, or if the rickshaw driver got paid. Rickshaw drivers are inclined at times to be violent, but then so are inmates of mental hospitals. Anyway, George seems to have no memory of that incident.

Three days later, I received word from the hospital that he had returned of his own accord, boasting that he had hit a century—so presumably, he had participated in some form of match or the other.

*

All's well that ends well, or so I like to think. Cousin George was not usually a violent man, but I have a funny feeling about the rickshaw driver. I never saw him again in Delhi, and unless he moved elsewhere, I'm afraid his disappearance might well be connected with Cousin George's rickshaw ride. After all, the Jamuna is very near Kotla.

The Fight

Ranji had been less than a month in Rajpur when he discovered the pool in the forest. It was the height of summer, and his school had not yet opened, and, having as yet made no friends in this semi-hill station, he wandered about a good deal by himself into the hills and forests that stretched away interminably on all sides of the town. It was hot, very hot, at that time of the year, and Ranji walked about in his vest and shorts, his brown feet white with the chalky dust that flew up from the ground. The earth was parched, the grass brown, the trees listless, hardly stirring, waiting for a cool wind or a refreshing shower of rain.

It was on such a day—a hot, tired day—that Ranji found the pool in the forest. The water had a gentle translucency, and you could see the smooth, round pebbles at the bottom of the pool. A small stream emerged from a cluster of rocks to feed the pool. During the monsoon, this stream would be a gushing torrent, cascading down from the hills, but during the summer, it was barely a trickle. The rocks, however, held the water in the pool, and it did not dry up like the pools in the plains.

When Ranji saw the pool, he did not hesitate to get into it.

He had often gone swimming, alone or with friends, when he had lived with his parents in a thirsty town in the middle of the Rajputana desert. There, he had known only sticky, muddy pools, where buffaloes wallowed and women washed clothes. He had never seen a pool like this—so clean and cold and inviting. He threw off all his clothes, as he had done when he went swimming in the plains, and leapt into the water. His limbs were supple, free of any fat, and his dark body glistened in patches of sunlit water.

The next day he came again to quench his body in the cool waters of the forest pool. He was there for almost an hour, sliding in and out of the limpid green water, or lying stretched out on the smooth yellow rocks in the shade of broad-leaved sal trees. It was while he lay thus, naked on a rock, that he noticed another boy standing a little distance away, staring at him in a rather hostile manner. The other boy was a little older than Ranji, taller, thickset, with a broad nose and thick, red lips. He had only just noticed Ranji, and he stood at the edge of the pool, wearing a pair of bathing shorts, waiting for Ranji to explain himself.

When Ranji did not say anything, the other called out, 'What are you doing here, Mister?'

Ranji, who was prepared to be friendly, was taken aback at the hostility of the other's tone.

'I am swimming,' he replied. 'Why don't you join me?'

'I always swim alone,' said the other. 'This is my pool, I did not invite you here. And why are you not wearing any clothes?'

'It is not your business if I do not wear clothes. I have nothing to be ashamed of.'

'You skinny fellow, put on your clothes.'

'Fat fool, take yours off.'

This was too much for the stranger to tolerate. He strode up to Ranji, who still sat on the rock and, planting his broad feet firmly on the sand, said (as though this would settle the matter once and for all), 'Don't you know I am a Punjabi? I do not take replies from villagers like you!'

'So you like to fight with villagers?' said Ranji. 'Well, I am not a villager. I am a Rajput!'

'I am a Punjabi!'

'I am a Rajput!'

They had reached an impasse. One had said he was a Punjabi, the other had proclaimed himself a Rajput. There was little else that could be said.

'You understand that I am a Punjabi?' said the stranger, feeling that perhaps this information had not penetrated Ranji's head.

'I have heard you say it three times,' replied Ranji.

'Then why are you not running away?'

'I am waiting for *you* to run away!'

'I will have to beat you,' said the stranger, assuming a violent attitude, showing Ranji the palm of his hand.

'I am waiting to see you do it,' said Ranji.

'You will see me do it,' said the other boy.

Ranji waited. The other boy made a strange hissing sound. They stared each other in the eye for almost a minute. Then the Punjabi boy slapped Ranji across the face with all the force he could muster. Ranji staggered, feeling quite dizzy. There were thick red finger marks on his cheek.

'There you are!' exclaimed his assailant. 'Will you be off now?'

51

For answer, Ranji swung his arm up and pushed a hard, bony fist into the other's face.

And then they were at each other's throats, swaying on the rock, tumbling on to the sand, rolling over and over, their legs and arms locked in a desperate, violent struggle. Gasping and cursing, clawing and slapping, they rolled right into the shallows of the pool.

Even in the water the fight continued as, spluttering and covered with mud, they groped for each other's head and throat. But after five minutes of frenzied, unscientific struggle, neither boy had emerged victorious. Their bodies heaving with exhaustion, they stood back from each other, making tremendous efforts to speak.

'Now—now do you realize—I am a Punjabi?' gasped the stranger.

'Do you know I am a Rajput?' said Ranji with difficulty.

They gave a moment's consideration to each other's answers and, in that moment of silence, there was only their heavy breathing and the rapid beating of their hearts.

'Then you will not leave the pool?' asked the Punjabi boy.

'I will not leave it,' said Ranji.

'Then we shall have to continue the fight,' said the other.

'All right,' said Ranji.

But neither boy moved, neither took the initiative. The Punjabi boy had an inspiration.

'We will continue the fight tomorrow,' he said. 'If you dare to come here again tomorrow, we will continue this fight, and I will not show you mercy as I have done today.'

'I will come tomorrow,' said Ranji. 'I will be ready for you.'

They turned from each other then and, going to their respective rocks, put on their clothes, and left the forest by different routes.

When Ranji got home, he found it difficult to explain the cuts and bruises that showed on his face, legs and arms. It was difficult to conceal the fact that he had been in an unusually violent fight, and his mother insisted on his staying at home for the rest of the day. That evening, though, he slipped out of the house and went to the bazaar, where he found comfort and solace in a bottle of vividly coloured lemonade and a banana-leaf full of hot, sweet jalebis. He had just finished the lemonade when he saw his adversary coming down the road. Ranji's first impulse was to turn away and look elsewhere, his second to throw the lemonade bottle at his enemy. But he did neither of these things. Instead, he stood his ground and scowled at his passing adversary. And the Punjabi boy said nothing either, but scowled back with equal ferocity.

The next day was as hot as the previous one. Ranji felt weak and lazy and not at all eager for a fight. His body was stiff and sore after the previous day's encounter. But he could not refuse the challenge. Not to turn up at the pool would be an acknowledgement of defeat. From the way he felt just then, he knew he would be beaten in another fight. But he could not acquiesce in his own defeat. He must defy his enemy to the last, or outwit him, for only then could he gain his respect. If he surrendered now, he would be beaten for all time; but to fight and be beaten today left him free to fight and be beaten again. As long as he fought, he had a right to the pool in the forest.

Ranji was half hoping that the Punjabi boy would have forgotten the challenge, but these hopes were dashed when he saw his opponent sitting, stripped to the waist, on a rock on the other side of the pool. The Punjabi boy was rubbing oil on his body, massaging it into his broad thighs. He saw Ranji beneath the sal trees, and called a challenge across the waters of the pool.

'Come over on this side and fight!' he shouted.

But Ranji was not going to submit to any conditions laid down by his opponent.

'Come *this* side and fight!' he shouted back with equal vigour.

'Swim across and fight me here!' called the other. 'Or perhaps you cannot swim the length of this pool?'

But Ranji could have swum the length of the pool a dozen times without tiring, and here he would show the Punjabi boy his superiority. So, slipping out of his vest and shorts, he dived straight into the water, cutting through it like a knife, and surfaced with hardly a splash. The Punjabi boy's mouth hung open in amazement.

'You can dive!' he exclaimed.

'It is easy,' said Ranji, treading water, waiting for a further challenge. 'Can't you dive?'

'No,' said the other. 'I jump straight in. But if you will tell me how, I will make a dive.'

'It is easy,' said Ranji. 'Stand on the rock, stretch your arms out and allow your head to displace your feet.'

The Punjabi boy stood up, stiff and straight, stretched out his arms, and threw himself into the water. He landed flat on his belly, with a crash that sent the birds screaming out of the trees.

Ranji dissolved into laughter.

'Are you trying to empty the pool?' he asked, as the Punjabi boy came to the surface, spouting water like a small whale.

'Wasn't it good?' asked the boy, evidently proud of his feat.

'Not very good,' said Ranji. 'You should have more practice. See, I will do it again.'

And pulling himself up on a rock, he executed another perfect dive. The other boy waited for him to come up, but, swimming under water, Ranji circled him and came upon him from behind.

'How did you do that?' asked the astonished youth.

'Can't you swim underwater?' asked Ranji.

'No, but I will try it.'

The Punjabi boy made a tremendous effort to plunge to the bottom of the pool and indeed he thought he had gone right down, though his bottom, like a duck's, remained above the surface.

Ranji, however, did not discourage him.

'It was not bad,' he said. 'But you need a lot of practice.'

'Will you teach me?' asked his enemy.

'If you like, I will teach you.'

'You must teach me. If you do not teach me, I will beat you. Will you come here every day and teach me?'

'If you like,' said Ranji. They had pulled themselves out of the water, and were sitting side by side on a smooth grey rock.

'My name is Daljit,' said the Punjabi boy. 'What is yours?'

'It is Ranji.'

'I am strong, am I not?' asked Daljit, bending his arm so that a ball of muscle stood up, stretching the white of his flesh.

'You are strong,' said Ranji. 'You are a real pahelwan.'

'One day I will be the world's champion wrestler,' said Daljit, slapping his thighs, which shook with the impact of his hand. He looked critically at Ranji's hard, thin body. 'You are quite strong yourself,' he conceded. 'But you are too bony. I know, you people do not eat enough. You must come and have your food with me. I drink one seer of milk every day. We have got our own cow! Be my friend, and I will make you a pahelwan like me! I know—if you teach me to dive and swim underwater, I will make you a pahelwan! That is fair, isn't it?'

'That is fair!' said Ranji, though he doubted if he was getting the better of the exchange.

Daljit put his arm around the younger boy and said, 'We are friends now, yes?'

They looked at each other with honest, unflinching eyes, and in that moment love and understanding were born.

'We are friends,' said Ranji.

The birds had settled again in their branches, and the pool was quiet and limpid in the shade of the sal trees.

'It is our pool,' said Daljit . 'Nobody else can come here without our permission. Who would dare?'

'Who would dare?' said Ranji, smiling with the knowledge that he had won the day.

Cricket—Field Placings

Long leg has cramp in one leg,
Short leg has a cramp in two;
Twelfth man is fielding at mid-off,
Because mid-on's gone off to the loo.
As short square leg has a long leg,
Long-off has been moved further off;
Silly-point goes back to gully
Cover-point backs off a pace or two.
Everyone is thinking of the drinks' trolley
When first slip lets a catch through his fingers,
Forgetting the old ball is now new.

Uncle Ken on the Job

'We'll have to do something about Uncle Ken,' said Granny to the world at large.

I was in the kitchen with her, shelling peas and popping a few into my mouth now and then. Suzie, the Siamese cat, sat on the sideboard, patiently watching Granny prepare an Irish stew. Suzie liked Irish stew.

'It's not that I mind him staying,' said Granny, 'and I don't want any money from him, either. But it isn't healthy for a young man to remain idle for so long.'

'Is Uncle Ken a young man, Gran?'

'He's forty. Everyone says he'll improve as he grows up.'

'He could go and live with Aunt Mabel.'

'He *does* go and live with Aunt Mabel. He also lives with Aunt Emily and Aunt Beryl. That's his trouble — he has too many doting sisters ready to put him up and put up with him . . . Their husbands are all quite well off and can afford to have him now and then. So our Ken spends three months with Mabel, three months with Beryl, three months with me. That way he gets through the year as everyone's guest and doesn't have to worry about making a living.'

'He's lucky in a way,' I said.

'His luck won't last for ever. Already Mabel is talking of going to New Zealand. And once India is free — in just a year or two from now — Emily and Beryl will probably go off to England, because their husbands are in the army and all the British officers will be leaving.'

'Can't Uncle Ken follow them to England?'

'He knows he'll have to start working if he goes there. When your aunts find they have to manage without servants, they won't be ready to keep Ken for long periods. In any case, who's going to pay his fare to England or New Zealand?'

'If he can't go, he'll stay here with you, Granny. You'll be here, won't you?'

'Not for ever. Only while I live.'

'You won't go to England?'

'No, I've grown up here. I'm like the trees. I've taken root, I won't be going away—not until, like an old tree, I'm without any more leaves . . . You'll go, though, when you are bigger. You'll probably finish your schooling abroad.'

'I'd rather finish it here. I want to spend all my holidays with you. If I go away, who'll look after you when you grow old?'

'I'm old already. Over sixty.'

'Is that very old? It's only a little older than Uncle Ken. And how will you look after him when you're *really* old?'

'He can look after himself if he tries. And it's time he started. It's time he took a job.'

I pondered on the problem. I could think of nothing that would suit Uncle Ken—or rather, I could think of no one who would find him suitable. It was Ayah who made a suggestion.

'The Maharani of Jetpur needs a tutor for her children,' she said. 'Just a boy and a girl.'

'How do you know?' asked Granny.

'I heard it from their ayah. The pay is two hundred rupees a month, and there is not much work—only two hours every morning.'

'That should suit Uncle Ken,' I said.

'Yes, it's a good idea,' said Granny. 'We'll have to talk him into applying. He ought to go over and see them. The Maharani is a good person to work for.'

Uncle Ken agreed to go over and inquire about the job. The Maharani was out when he called, but he was interviewed by the Maharaja.

'Do you play tennis?' asked the Maharaja.

'Yes,' said Uncle Ken, who remembered having played a bit of tennis when he was a schoolboy.

'In that case, the job's yours. I've been looking for a fourth player for a doubles match . . . By the way, were you at Cambridge?'

'No, I was at Oxford,' said Uncle Ken.

The Maharaja was impressed. An Oxford man who could play tennis was just the sort of tutor he wanted for his children.

When Uncle Ken told Granny about the interview, she said, 'But you haven't been to Oxford, Ken. How could you say that?'

'Of course I have been to Oxford. Don't you remember? I spent two years there with your brother Jim!'

'Yes, but you were helping him in his pub in the town. You weren't at the University.'

'Well, the Maharaja never asked me if I had been to the University. He asked me if I was at Cambridge, and I said no, I was at Oxford, which was perfectly true. He didn't ask me what I was doing at Oxford. What difference does it make?' And he strolled off, whistling.

To our surprise, Uncle Ken was a great success in his job. In the beginning, anyway.

The Maharaja was such a poor tennis player that he was delighted to discover that there was someone who was even worse. So, instead of becoming a doubles partner for the Maharaja, Uncle Ken became his favourite singles opponent. As long as he could keep losing to His Highness, Uncle Ken's job was safe.

In between tennis matches and accompanying his employer on duck shoots, Uncle Ken squeezed in a few lessons for the children, teaching them reading, writing and arithmetic. Sometimes he took me along, so that I could tell him when he got his sums wrong. Uncle Ken wasn't very good at subtraction, although he could add fairly well.

The Maharaja's children were younger than me. Uncle Ken would leave me with them, saying, 'Just see that they do their sums properly, Ruskin,' and he would stroll off to the tennis courts, hands in his pockets, whistling tunelessly.

POK!

Even if his pupils had different answers to the same sum, he would give both of them an encouraging pat, saying, 'Excellent, excellent. I'm glad to see both of you trying so hard. One of you is right and one of you is wrong, but as I don't want to discourage either of you, I won't say who's right and who's wrong!'

But afterwards, on the way home, he'd ask me, 'Which was the right answer, Ruskin?'

Uncle Ken always maintained that he would never have lost his job if he hadn't beaten the Maharaja at tennis.

Not that Uncle Ken had any intention of winning. But by playing occasional games with the Maharaja's secretaries and guests, his tennis had improved and so, try as hard as he might to lose, he couldn't help winning a match against his employer.

The Maharaja was furious.

'Mr Clerke,' he said sternly, 'I don't think you realize the importance of losing. We can't all win, you know. Where would the world be without losers?'

'I'm terribly sorry,' said Uncle Ken. 'It was just a fluke, your Highness.'

The Maharaja accepted Uncle Ken's apologies; but a week later it happened again. Kenneth Clerke won and the Maharaja stormed off the court without saying a word. The following day he turned up at lesson time. As usual Uncle Ken and the children were engaged in a game of noughts and crosses.

'We won't be requiring your services from tomorrow, Mr Clerke. I've asked my secretary to give you a month's salary in lieu of notice.'

Uncle Ken came home with his hands in his pockets, whistling cheerfully.

'You're early,' said Granny.

'They don't need me any more,' said Uncle Ken.

'Oh well, never mind. Come in and have your tea.'

Granny must have known the job wouldn't last very long. And she wasn't one to nag. As she said later, 'At least he tried. And it lasted longer than most of his jobs—two months.'

Uncle Ken at the Wicket

Although restored to the Maharaja's favour by losing to him at tennis, Uncle Ken was still without a job.

Granny refused to let him take the Hillman out again and so he decided to sulk. He said it was all Grandfather's fault for not seeing to the steering wheel ten years ago, while he was still alive. Uncle Ken went on a hunger strike for two hours (between tiffin and tea), and we did not hear him whistle for several days.

'The blessedness of silence,' said Granny.

And then he announced that he was going to Lucknow to stay with Aunt Emily.

'She has three children and a school to look after,' said Granny. 'Don't stay too long.'

'She doesn't mind how long I stay,' said Uncle Ken and off he went.

His visit to Lucknow was a memorable one, and we only heard about it much later.

When Uncle Ken got down at Lucknow station, he found himself surrounded by a large crowd, everyone waving to him and shouting words of welcome in Hindi, Urdu and English. Before he could make out what it was all about, he was smothered by garlands of marigolds. A young man came forward and announced, 'The Gomti Cricketing Association welcomes you to the historical city of Lucknow,' and promptly led Uncle Ken out of the station to a waiting car.

It was only when the car drove into the sports stadium that Uncle Ken realized that he was expected to play in a cricket match.

This is what had happened.

Bruce Hallam, the famous English cricketer, was touring India and had agreed to play in a charity match at Lucknow. But the previous evening, in Delhi, Bruce had gone to bed with an upset stomach and hadn't been able to get up in time to catch the train. A telegram was sent to the organizers of the match in Lucknow; but, like many a telegram, it did

not reach its destination. The cricket fans of Lucknow had arrived at the station in droves to welcome the great cricketer. And by a strange coincidence, Uncle Ken bore a startling resemblance to Bruce Hallam; even the bald patch on the crown of his head was exactly like Hallam's. Hence the muddle. And, of course, Uncle Ken was always happy to enter into the spirit of a muddle.

Having received from the Gomti Cricketing Association a rousing reception and a magnificent breakfast at the stadium, he felt that it would be very unsporting on his part if he refused to play cricket for them. 'If I can hit a tennis ball,' he mused, 'I ought to be able to hit a cricket ball.' And luckily there was a blazer and a pair of white flannels in his suitcase.

The Gomti team won the toss and decided to bat. Uncle Ken was expected to go in at Number 3, Bruce Hallam's normal position. And he soon found himself walking to the wicket, wondering why on earth no one had as yet invented a more comfortable kind of pad.

The first ball he received was short-pitched, and he was able to deal with it in tennis fashion, swatting it to the mid-wicket boundary. He got no runs, but the crowd cheered.

The next ball took Uncle Ken on the pad. He was right in front of his wicket and should have been given out lbw. But the umpire hesitated to raise his finger. After all, hundreds of people had paid good money to see Bruce Hallam play, and it would have been a shame to disappoint them. 'Not out,' said the umpire.

The third ball took the edge of Uncle Ken's bat and sped through the slips.

'Lovely shot!' exclaimed an elderly gentleman in the pavilion.

'A classic late cut,' said another.

The ball reached the boundary and Uncle Ken had four runs to his name. Then it was 'over', and the other batsman had to face the bowling. He took a run off the first ball and called for a second run.

Uncle Ken thought one run was more than enough. Why go charging up and down the wicket like a mad man? However, he couldn't refuse to run, and he was halfway down the pitch when the fielder's throw hit the wicket. Uncle Ken was run-out by yards. There could be no doubt about it this time.

He returned to the pavilion to the sympathetic applause of the crowd.

'Not his fault,' said the elderly gentleman. 'The other chap shouldn't have called. There wasn't a run there. Still, it was worth coming here all the way from Kanpur if only to see that superb late cut . . .'

*

Uncle Ken enjoyed a hearty tiffin-box lunch (at noon), and then, realizing that the Gomti team would probably have to be in the field for most of the afternoon—more running about!—he slipped out of the pavilion, left the stadium, and took a tonga to Aunt Emily's house in the cantonment.

He was just in time for a second lunch (at one o'clock) with Aunt Emily's family: and it was presumed at the stadium that Bruce Hallam had left early to catch the train to Allahabad, where he was expected to play in another charity match.

Aunt Emily, a forceful woman, fed Uncle Ken for a week, and then put him to work in the boys' dormitory of her school. It was several months before he was able to save up enough money to run away and return to Granny's place.

But he had the satisfaction of knowing that he had helped the great Bruce Hallam to add another four runs to his grand aggregate. The scorebook of the

Gomti Cricketing Association had recorded his feat for all time:

'B. Hallam run-out 4.'

The Gomti team lost the match. But, as Uncle Ken would readily admit, where would we be without losers?

A Bicycle Ride with Uncle Ken

Kissing a girl while sharing a bicycle with her is no easy task, but I managed it when I was thirteen and my cousin Melanie was fourteen. Of course, we both fell off in the process, and landed in one of Granny's flower beds where we were well cushioned by her nasturtiums.

I was a clumsy boy, always falling off bicycles, and Cousin Melanie was teaching me to ride properly, making me sit on the front seat while she guided the infernal machine from the carrier seat. The kiss was purely experimental. I had not kissed a girl before, and as Cousin Melanie seemed eminently kissable, I thought I'd start with her. I waited until we were stationary, and she was instructing me on the intricacies of the cycle chain, and then I gave her a hurried kiss on the cheek. She was so startled that she fell backwards, taking me and the bicycle with her.

Later, she reported me to Granny, who said, 'We'll have to keep an eye on that boy. He's showing signs of a dissolute nature.'

'What's dissolute, Uncle Ken?' I asked my favourite uncle.

'It means you're going to the dogs. You're not supposed to kiss your cousin.'

'Can I kiss other girls?'

'Only if they are willing.'

'Did you ever kiss a girl, Uncle Ken?'

Uncle Ken blushed. 'Er . . . well . . . a long time ago.'

'Tell me about it.'

'Another time.'

'No, tell me now. How old were you?'

'About twenty.'

'And how old was she?'

'A bit younger.'

'And what happened?'

'We went cycling together. I was staying in Agra, when your grandfather worked there with the railways. Daisy's father was an engine driver. But she didn't like engines; they left her covered with soot. Everyone had a bicycle in those days, only the very rich had cars. And the cars could not keep up with the bicycles.

'We lived in the cantonment, where the roads were straight and wide. Daisy and I went on cycle rides to Fatehpur Sikri and Sikandra and of course the Taj Mahal, and one evening we saw the Taj Mahal by moonlight and it made us very romantic, and when I saw her home we kissed under the Asoka trees.'

'I didn't know you were so romantic, Uncle Ken. Why didn't you marry Daisy?'

'I didn't have a job. She said she'd wait until I got one, but after two years, she got tired of waiting. She married a ticket inspector.'

'Such a sad story,' I said. 'And you still don't have a job.'

Uncle Ken had been through various jobs—private tutor, salesman, shop assistant, hotel manager (until he brought about the closure of the hotel), and cricket coach, this last on the strength of bearing a close resemblance to Bruce Hallam—but at present he was unemployed, and only too ready to put his vast experience of life at my disposal.

Not only did he teach me to ride a bicycle but also accompanied me on cycle rides around Dehra and along the lanes and country roads outside the town.

A bicycle provides its rider with a great amount of freedom. A car will take you further but the fact that you're sitting in a confined space detracts from the freedom of the open spaces and unfamiliar roads. On a cycle you can feel the breeze on your face, smell the mango trees in blossom, slow down and gaze at the buffaloes wading in their ponds, or just stop anywhere and get down and enjoy a cup of tea or a glass of sugar cane juice. Foot-slogging takes time, and cars are too fast—everything whizzes past you before you can take a second look—and car drivers hate having to stop; they are intent only on reaching their destinations in good time. But a bicycle is just right for someone who likes to take a leisurely look at the world as well as to give the world a chance to look at him.

Uncle Ken and I had some exhilarating bicycle rides during my winter holidays, and the most memorable of these was our unplanned visit to a certain 'Rest Home' situated on the outskirts of the town. It isn't there now, so don't go looking for it.

We had cycled quite far that day, and were tired and thirsty. There was no sign of a tea shop on that particular road, but when we arrived at the open gate of an impressive building with a signboard saying 'Rest and Recuperation Centre', we presumed it was a hotel

or hostelry of sorts and rode straight into the premises. There was an extensive lawn to one side, surrounded by neat hedges and flowering shrubs. A number of people were strolling about on the lawn; some were sitting on benches; one or two were straddling a wall, talking to themselves; another was standing alone singing to a non-existent audience. Some were Europeans; a few were Indians.

We left our cycles in the porch and went in search of refreshment. A lady in a white sari gave us cool water from a surahi and told us we could wait on a bench just outside their office. But Uncle Ken said we'd prefer to meet some of the guests, and led me across the lawn to where the singer was practising his notes. He was a florid gentleman, heavily-built.

'Do you like my singing?' he asked, as we came up.

'Wonderful!' exclaimed Uncle Ken. 'You sing like Caruso.'

'I am Caruso!' affirmed the tenor, and let rip the opening notes of a famous operatic aria. '*Your tiny hand is frozen,*' he sang, although it was an unusually warm day.

We hurried on, and met an elegant couple who were parading up and down the lawn, waving their hands to an invisible crowd.

'Good day to you, gentlemen,' said the flamboyant individual. 'You're the ambassadors from Sweden, I suppose.'

'If you so wish,' said Uncle Ken gallantly. 'And I have the honour of speaking to—?'

'The Emperor Napoleon, of course.'

'Of course. And this must be the Empress Josephine.' Uncle Ken bowed to the lady beside him.

'Actually, his Marie Waleska,' said Napoleon. 'Josephine is indisposed today.'

I was beginning to feel like Alice at the Mad Hatter's tea party, and began tugging at Uncle Ken's coat sleeve, whispering that we were getting late for lunch.

A turbaned warrior with a tremendous moustache loomed in front of us. 'I'm Prithviraj Chauhan,' he announced. 'And I invite you to dinner at my palace.'

'Everyone's royalty here,' observed Uncle Ken.

'It's such a privilege to be with you.'

'Me too,' I put in nervously.

'Come with me, boy, and I'll introduce you to the others.' Prithviraj Chauhan took me by the hand and began guiding me across the lawn. 'There are many famous men and women here. That's Marco Polo over there. He's just back from China. And if you don't care for Caruso's signing, there's Tansen under that tamarind tree. Tamarind leaves are good for the voice, you know that of course. And that fashionable gentleman there, he's Lord Curzon, who used to be a viceroy. He's talking to the Sultan of Marrakesh. Come along, I'll introduce you to them . . . You're the young prince of Denmark, aren't you?'

'Hamlet himself,' said Uncle Ken with a wink.

Before I could refute any claims to royalty, we were intercepted by a white-coated gentleman accompanied by a white-coated assistant. They looked as though they were in charge.

'And what are you doing here, young man?' asked the senior of the two.

'I'm with my uncle,' I said, gesturing towards Uncle Ken, who approached and gave the in-charge an affable handshake.

'And you must be Dr Freud,' said Uncle Ken. 'I must say this is a jolly sort of place.'

'Actually, I'm Dr Goel. You must be the new patient we were expecting. But they should have sent you over with someone a little older than this boy. Never mind, come along to the office and we'll have you admitted.'

Uncle Ken and I both protested that we were not potential patients but had entered the grounds by mistake. We had our bicycles to prove it! But Dr Goel was having nothing of this deception. He and his assistant linked arms with Uncle Ken and marched him off to the office, while I trailed behind, wondering if I should get on my bicycle and rush back to Granny with the terrible news that Uncle Ken had been incarcerated in a lunatic asylum.

Just then an ambulance arrived with the real patient, a school principal suffering from a persecution complex. He kept shouting that he was perfectly sane, and that his entire staff had plotted to have him put away. This might well have been true, as the staff was there in force to make sure he did not escape.

Dr Goel apologized to Uncle Ken. Uncle Ken apologized to Dr Goel. The good doctor even accompanied us to the gate. He shook hands with Uncle Ken and said, 'I have a feeling we'll see you here again.' He looked hard at my uncle and added, 'I think I've seen you before, sir. What did you say your name was?'

'Bruce Hallam,' said Uncle Ken mischievously, and rode away before they changed their minds and kept him in their 'Rest Home'.

The Long Day

Suraj was awakened by the sound of his mother busying herself in the kitchen. He lay in bed, looking through the open window at the sky getting lighter and the dawn pushing its way into the room. He knew there was something important about this new day, but for some time he couldn't remember what it was. Then, as the room cleared, his mind cleared. His school report would be arriving in the post.

Suraj knew he had failed. The class teacher had told him so. But his mother would only know of it when she read the report, and Suraj did not want to be in the house when she received it. He was sure it would be arriving today. So he had told his mother that he would be having his midday meal with his friend

Somi—who wasn't even in town at the moment—and would be home only for the evening meal. By the time, he hoped, his mother would have recovered from the shock. He was glad his father was away on tour.

He slipped out of bed and went to the kitchen. His mother was surprised to see him up so early.

'I'm going for a walk, Ma,' he said, 'and then I'll go on to Somi's house.'

'Well, have your bath first and put something in your stomach.'

Suraj went to the tap in the courtyard and took a quick bath. He put on a clean shirt and shorts. Carelessly he brushed his thick, curly hair, knowing he couldn't bring much order to its wildness. Then he gulped down a glass of milk and hurried out of the house. The postman wouldn't arrive for a couple of hours, but Suraj felt that the earlier he started the better. His mother was surprised and pleased to see him up and about so early.

Suraj went out on to the maidan and still the sun had not risen. The maidan was an open area of grass, about a hundred square metres, and from the middle of it could be seen the mountains, range upon range of them, stepping into the sky. A game of football was in progress, and one of the players called out to Suraj to

join them. Suraj said he wouldn't play for more than ten minutes, because he had some business to attend to; he kicked off his chappals and ran barefoot after the ball. Everyone was playing barefoot. It was an informal game, and the players were of all ages and sizes, from bearded Sikhs to small boys of six or seven. Suraj ran all over the place without actually getting in touch with the ball—he wasn't much good at football—and finally got into a scramble before the goal, fell and scratched his knee. He retired from the game sooner than he had intended.

The scratch wasn't bad but there was some blood on the knee. He wiped it clean with his handkerchief and limped off the maidan. He went in the direction of the railway station, but not through the bazaar. He went by way of the canal, which came from the foot of the nearest mountain, flowed through the town and down to the river. Beside the canal were the washerwomen, scrubbing and beating out clothes on the stone banks.

The canal was only a metre wide but, due to recent rains, the current was swift and noisy. Suraj stood on the bank, watching the rush of water. There was an inlet at the one place, and here some children were bathing, and some were rushing up and down the bank, wearing nothing at all, shouting to each other in high spirits. Suraj felt like taking a dip too, but he did not know any of the children here; most of them were from very poor families. Hands in pockets, he walked along the canal banks.

The sun had risen and was pouring through the branches of the trees and lined the road. The leaves made shadowy patterns on the ground. Suraj tried hard not to think of his school report, but he knew that at any moment now the postman would be handing over a long brown envelope to his mother. He tried to imagine his mother's expression when she read the report; but the more he tried to picture her face, the more certain he was that, on knowing his result, she would show no expression at all. And having no expression on her face was much worse than having one.

Suraj heard the whistle of a train, and knew he was not far from the station. He cut through a field, climbed a hillock and ran down the slope until he was near the railway tracks. Here came the train, screeching and puffing: in the distance, a big black beetle, and then, when the carriages swung into sight, a centipede…

Suraj stood a good twenty metres away from the lines, on the slope of the hill. As the train passed, he pulled the handkerchief off his knees and began to wave it furiously. There was something about passing trains that filled him with awe and excitement. All those passengers, with mysterious lives and mysterious destinations, were people he wanted to know, people whose mysteries he wanted to unfold. He had been in a train recently, when his parents had taken him to bathe in the sacred river, Ganga, at Hardwar. He wished he could be in a train now; or better still be an engine driver, with no more books and teachers and school reports. He did not know of any thirteen-year-old engine drivers, but he saw himself driving the engine, shouting orders to the stoker; it made him feel powerful to be in control of the mighty steam engine.

Someone—another boy—returned his wave, and the two waved at each other for a few seconds, and then the train had passed, its smoke spiralling backwards.

Suraj felt a little lonely now. Somehow, the passing of the train left him with a feeling of being alone in a wide, empty world. He was feeling hungry too. He went back to the field where he had seen some litchi trees, climbed on to one of them, and began plucking and peeling and eating the juicy red-skinned fruit. No one seemed to own the litchi trees because, although a dog appeared below and began barking, no none else appeared. Suraj kept spitting litchi seeds at the dog, and the dog kept barking at him. Eventually the dog lost interest and slunk off.

Suraj began to feel drowsy in the afternoon heat. The litchi trees offered a lot of shade, so he came down from the tree and sat on the grass, his back resting against the tree trunk. A mynah came hopping up to his feet and looked at him curiously, its head to one side.

Insects kept buzzing around Suraj. He swiped at them once or twice, but then couldn't make the effort to keep swiping. He opened his shirt buttons. The air was very hot, very still; the only sound was the faint buzzing of the insects. His head fell forward on his chest.

He opened his eyes to find himself being shaken, and looked up into the round, cheerful face of his friend Ranji.

'What are you doing, sleeping here?' asked Ranji, who was a couple of years younger than Suraj. 'Have you run away from home?'

'Not yet,' said Suraj. 'And what are *you* doing here?'

'Came for litchis.'

'So did I.'

They sat together for a while and talked and ate litchis. Then Ranji suggested that they visit the bazaar to eat pakoras.

'I haven't any money,' said Suraj.

'That doesn't matter,' said Ranji, who always seemed to be in funds. 'I have two rupees.'

So they walked to the bazaar. They crossed the field, walked back past the canal, skirted the maidan, came to the clock tower and entered the bazaar.

The evening crowd had just begun to fill the road, and there was a lot of bustle and noise: the street vendors called their wares in high, strident voices; children shouted and women bargained. There was a medley of smells and aromas coming from the little restaurants and sweet shops, and a riot of colour in the bangle and kite shops. Suraj and Ranji ate their pakoras, felt thirsty, and gazed at the rows and rows of coloured bottles at the cold drinks shop that were available. But they had already finished the two rupees, so there was nothing for them to do but quench their thirst at the municipal tap.

Afterwards they wandered down the crowded street, examining the shopfronts, commenting on the passers-by, and every now and then greeting some friend or acquaintance. Darkness came on suddenly, and then the bazaar was lit up, the big shops with bright electric and neon lights, the street vendors with oil lamps. The bazaar at night was even more exciting than during the day.

They traversed the bazaar from end to end and, when they were at the clock tower again, Ranji said he had to go home, and left Suraj. It was nearing Suraj's dinner time and so, unwillingly, he too turned homewards. He did not want it to appear that he was deliberately staying out late because of the school report.

The lights were on in the front room when he got home. He waited outside, secure in the darkness of the veranda, watching the lighted room. His mother would be waiting for him, she would probably have the report in her hand or on the kitchen shelf, and she would have lots of questions to ask him.

All the cares in the world seemed to descend on Suraj as he crept into the house.

'You're late,' said his mother. 'Come and have your food.'

Suraj said nothing, but removed his shoes outside the kitchen and sat down cross-legged on the kitchen floor, which was where he took his meals. He was tired and hungry. He no longer cared about anything else.

'One of your class-fellows dropped in,' said his mother. He said your reports were sent out today. They'll arrive tomorrow.'

Tomorrow! Suraj felt a great surge of relief.

But then, just as suddenly, his spirits fell again.

Tomorrow. . . a further postponement of the dreaded moment, another night and another morning. . . something would have to be done about it!

'Ma,' he said abruptly. 'Somi has asked me to his house again tomorrow.'

'I don't know how his mother puts up with you so often,' said Suraj's mother.

Suraj lay awake in bed, planning the morrow's activities: a game of cricket or football on the maidan; perhaps a dip in the canal; a half-hour of watching the trains thunder past; and in the evening an hour in the bazaar, among the kites and balloons and rose-coloured fizzy drinks and round, dripping syrupy sweets. . .

Perhaps in the morning, he could persuade his mother to give him two or three rupees. . . It would be his last rupee for quite some time.

Riding Through the Flames

I

As Romi was about to mount his bicycle, he saw smoke rising from behind the distant line of trees.

'It looks like a forest fire,' said Prem, his friend and classmate.

'It's well to the east,' said Romi. 'Nowhere near the road.'

'There's a strong wind,' said Prem, looking at the dry leaves swirling across the road.

It was the middle of May, and it hadn't rained for several weeks. The grass was brown, the leaves of the trees covered with dust. Even though it was getting on to six o'clock in the evening, the boys' shirts were damp with sweat.

'It will be getting dark soon,' said Prem. 'You'd better spend the night at my house.'

'No, I said I'd be home tonight. My father isn't keeping well. The doctor has given me some pills for him.'

'You'd better hurry, then. That fire seems to be spreading.'

'Oh, it's far off. It will take me only forty minutes to ride through the forest. Bye, Prem—see you tomorrow!'

Romi mounted his bicycle and pedalled off down the main road of the village, scattering stray hens, stray dogs and stray villagers.

'Hey, look where you're going!' shouted an angry villager, leaping out of the way of the oncoming bicycle. 'Do you think you own the road?'

'Of course I own it,' called Romi cheerfully, and cycled on.

His own village lay about seven miles away, on the other side of the forest; but there was only a primary school in his village, and Romi was now in high school. His father, who was a fairly wealthy sugar cane farmer, had only recently bought him the bicycle. Romi didn't care too much for school and felt there weren't enough holidays but he enjoyed the long rides, and he got on well with his classmates.

He might have stayed the night with Prem had it not been for the pills which the vaid—the village doctor—had given him for his father.

Romi's father was suffering from back trouble, and the pills had been specially prepared from local herbs.

Having been given such a fine bicycle, Romi felt that the least he could do in return was to get those pills to his father as early as possible.

He put his head down and rode swiftly out of the village. Ahead of him, the smoke rose from the burning forest and the sky glowed red.

II

He had soon left the village far behind. There was a slight climb, and Romi had to push harder on the pedals to get over the rise. Once over the top, the road went winding down to the edge of the forest.

This was the part Romi enjoyed the most. He relaxed, stopped pedalling, and allowed the bicycle to glide gently down the slope. Soon the wind was rushing past him, blowing his hair about his face and making his shirt billow out behind him. He burst into song.

A dog from the village ran beside him, barking furiously.

Romi shouted to the dog, encouraging him in the race.

Then the road straightened out, and Romi began pedalling again.

The dog, seeing the forest ahead, turned back to the village. It was afraid of the forest.

The smoke was thicker now, and Romi caught the smell of burning timber. But ahead of him the road was clear. He rode on.

It was a rough, dusty road, cut straight through the forest. Tall trees grew on either side, cutting off the last of the daylight. But the spreading glow of the fire on the right lit up the road, and giant tree-shadows danced before the boy on the bicycle.

Usually the road was deserted. This evening it was alive with wild creatures fleeing from the forest fire.

The first animal that Romi saw was a hare, leaping across the road in front of him. It was followed by several more hares. Then a band of monkeys streamed across, chattering excitedly.

They'll be safe on the other side, thought Romi. The fire won't cross the road.

But it was coming closer. And realizing this, Romi pedalled harder. In half an hour he should be out of the forest.

Suddenly, from the side of the road, several pheasants rose in the air, and with a *whoosh*, flew low across the path, just in front of the oncoming bicycle. Taken by surprise, Romi fell off. When he picked himself up and began brushing his clothes, he saw that his knee was bleeding. It wasn't a deep cut, but he allowed it to bleed a little, took out his handkerchief and bandaged his knee. Then he mounted the bicycle again.

He rode a bit slower now, because birds and animals kept coming out of the bushes.

Not only pheasants but smaller birds too were streaming across the road—parrots, jungle crows, owls, magpies—and the air was filled with their cries.

Everyone's on the move, thought Romi. It must be a really big fire.

He could see the flames now, reaching out from behind the trees on his right, and he could hear the crackling as the dry leaves caught fire. The air was hot on his face. Leaves, still alight or turning to cinders, floated past.

A herd of deer crossed the road and Romi had to stop until they had passed. Then he mounted again and rode on; but now, for the first time, he was feeling afraid.

III

From ahead came a faint clanging sound. It wasn't an animal sound, Romi was sure of that. A fire engine? There were no fire engines within fifty miles.

The clanging came nearer and Romi discovered that the noise came from a small boy who was running along the forest path, two milk cans clattering at his side.

'Teju!' called Romi, recognizing a boy from a neighbouring village. 'What are you doing out here?'

'Trying to get home, of course,' said Teju, panting along beside the bicycle.

'Jump on,' said Romi, stopping for him.

Teju was only eight or nine—a couple of years younger than Romi. He had come to deliver milk to some road-workers, but the workers had left at the first signs of the fire, and Teju was hurrying home with his cans still full of milk.

He got up on the crossbar of the bicycle, and Romi moved on again. He was quite used to carrying friends on the crossbar.

'Keep beating your milk cans,' said Romi. 'Like that, the animals will know we are coming. My bell doesn't make enough noise. I'm going to get a horn for my cycle!'

'I never knew there were so many animals in the jungle,' said Teju. 'I saw a python in the middle of the road. It stretched right across!'

'What did you do?'

'Just kept running and jumped right over it!'

Teju continued to chatter but Romi's thoughts were on the fire, which was much closer now. Flames shot up from the dry grass and ran up the trunks of trees and along the branches. Smoke billowed out above the forest.

Romi's eyes were smarting and his hair and eyebrows felt scorched. He was feeling tired but he couldn't stop now, he had to get beyond the range of the fire. Another ten or fifteen minutes of steady riding would get them to the small wooden bridge that spanned the little river separating the forest from the sugarcane fields.

Once across the river, they would be safe. The fire could not touch them on the other side because the forest ended at the river's edge. But could they get to the river in time?

IV

Clang, clang, clang, went Teju's milk cans. But the sounds of the fire grew louder too.

A tall silk cotton tree, its branches leaning across the road, had caught fire. They were almost beneath it when there was a crash and a burning branch fell to the ground a few yards in front of them.

The boys had to get off the bicycle and leave the road, forcing their way through a tangle of thorny bushes on the left, dragging and pushing at the bicycle and only returning to the road some distance ahead of the burning tree.

'We won't get out in time,' said Teju, back on the crossbar but feeling disheartened.

'Yes, we will,' said Romi, pedalling with all his might. 'The fire hasn't crossed the road as yet.'

Even as he spoke, he saw a small flame leap up from the grass on the left. It wouldn't be long before more sparks and burning leaves were blown across the road to kindle the grass on the other side.

'Oh, look!' exclaimed Romi, bringing the bicycle to a sudden stop.

'What's wrong now?' asked Teju, rubbing his sore eyes. And then, through the smoke, he saw what was stopping them.

An elephant was standing in the middle of the road.

Teju slipped off the crossbar, his cans rolling on the ground, bursting open and spilling their contents.

The elephant was about forty feet away. It moved about restlessly, its big ears flapping as it turned its head from side to side, wondering which way to go.

From far to the left, where the forest was still untouched, a herd of elephants moved towards the river. The leader of the herd raised his trunk and trumpeted a call. Hearing it, the elephant on the road raised its own trunk and trumpeted a reply. Then it shambled off into the forest, in the direction of the herd, leaving the way clear.

'Come, Teju, jump on!' urged Romi. 'We can't stay here much longer!'

V

Teju forgot about his milk cans and pulled himself up on the crossbar. Romi ran forward with the bicycle, to gain speed, and mounted swiftly. He kept, as far as possible to the left of the road, trying to ignore the flames, the crackling, the smoke and the scorching heat.

It seemed that all the animals who could get away had done so. The exodus across the road had stopped.

'We won't stop again,' said Romi, gritting his teeth. 'Not even for an elephant!'

'We're nearly there!' said Teju. He was perking up again.

A jackal, overcome by the heat and smoke, lay in the middle of the path, either dead or unconscious. Romi did not stop. He swerved round the animal. Then he put all his strength into one final effort.

He covered the last hundred yards at top speed, and then they were out of the forest, freewheeling down the sloping road to the river.

'Look!' shouted Teju. 'The bridge is on fire!'

Burning embers had floated down on to the small wooden bridge and the dry, ancient timber had quickly caught fire. It was now burning fiercely.

Romi did not hesitate. He left the road, riding the bicycle over sand and pebbles. Then with a rush they went down the riverbank and into the water.

The next thing they knew they were splashing around, trying to find each other in the darkness.

'Help!' cried Teju. 'I'm drowning!'

VI

'Don't be silly,' said Romi. 'The water isn't deep—it's only up to the knees. Come here and grab hold of me.'

Teju splashed across and grabbed Romi by the belt. 'The water's so cold,' he said, his teeth chattering.

'Do you want to go back and warm yourself?' asked Romi. 'Some people are never satisfied. Come on, help me get the bicycle up. It's down here, just where we are standing.'

Together they managed to heave the bicycle out of the water and stand it upright.

'Now sit on it,' said Romi. 'I'll push you across.'

'We'll be swept away,' said Teju.

'No, we won't. There's not much water in the river at this time of the year. But the current is quite strong in the middle, so sit still. All right?'

'All right,' said Teju nervously.

Romi began guiding the bicycle across the river, one hand on the seat and one hand on the handlebar. The river was shallow and sluggish in midsummer; even so, it was quite swift in the middle. But having got

safely out of the burning forest, Romi was in no mood to let a little river defeat him.

He kicked off his shoes, knowing they would be lost, and then gripping the smooth stones of the riverbed with his toes, he concentrated on keeping his balance and getting Teju and the bicycle through the middle of the stream. The water here came up to his waist, and the current would have been too strong for Teju. But when they reached the shallows, Teju got down and helped Romi push the bicycle.

They reached the opposite bank and sank down on the grass.

'We can rest now,' said Romi. 'But not all night — I've got some medicine to give my father.' He felt in his pockets and found that the pills, in their envelope, had turned to a soggy mess. 'Oh well, he has to take them with water anyway,' he said.

They watched the fire as it continued to pread through the forest. It had crossed the road down which they had come. The sky was a bright red, and the river reflected the colour of the sky.

Several elephants had found their way down to the river. They were cooling off by spraying water on each other with their trunks. Further downstream there were deer and other animals.

Romi and Teju looked at each other in the glow from the fire. They hadn't known each other very well before. But now they felt they had been friends for years.

'What are you thinking about?' asked Teju.

'I'm thinking,' said Romi, 'that even if the fire is out in a day or two, it will be a long time before the bridge is repaired. So I'm thinking it will be a nice long holiday from school!'

'But you can walk across the river,' said Teju. 'You just did it.'

'Impossible,' said Romi. 'It's much too fast.'

Boy Scouts Forever!

I was a Boy Scout once, although I couldn't tell a slip knot from a granny knot, or a reef knot from a thief knot, except that a thief knot was supposed to be used to tie up a thief, should you happen to catch one. I have never caught a thief, and wouldn't know what to do with one since I can't tie a knot. Just let him go with a warning, I suppose. Tell him to become a Boy Scout.

'Be prepared!' That's the Boy Scout motto. And a good one, too. But I never seem to be well prepared for anything, be it an exam or a journey or the roof blowing off my room. I get halfway through a speech and then forget what I have to say next. Or I make a new suit to attend a friend's wedding, and then turn up in my pyjamas.

So how did I, the most impractical of boys, become a Boy Scout? I was at boarding school in Simla when it happened.

Well, it seems a rumour had gone around the junior school (I was still a junior then) that I was a good cook. I had never cooked anything in my life, but of course I had spent a lot of time in the tuck shop making suggestions and advising Chippu, who ran the tuck shop, and encouraging him to make more and better samosas, jalebis, tikkees and pakoras. For my unwanted advice he would favour me with an occasional free samosa, so naturally I looked upon him as a friend and benefactor. With this qualification I was given a cookery badge and put in charge of our troop's supply of rations.

There were about twenty of us in our troop, and during the summer break our Scoutmaster, Mr Oliver, took us on a camping expedition to Tara Devi, a temple-crowned mountain a few miles outside Simla. That first night we were put to work, peeling potatoes, skinning onions, shelling peas and pounding masalas. These various ingredients being ready, I was asked—as the troop's cookery expert—what should be done with them.

'Put everything in that big *degchi*,' I ordered. 'Pour half a tin of ghee over the lot. Add some nettle leaves and cook for half an hour.'

When this was done, everyone had a taste, but the general opinion was that the dish lacked something.

'More salt,' I suggested.

More salt was added. It still lacked something.

'Add a cup of sugar,' I ordered.

Sugar was added to the concoction. But still it lacked something.

'We forgot to add tomatoes,' said Bimal, one of the Scouts.

'Never mind,' I said. 'We have tomato sauce. Add a bottle of tomato sauce!'

'How about some vinegar?' asked another boy.

'Just the thing,' I agreed. 'A cup of vinegar!'

'Now it's too sour,' said one of the tasters.

'What jam did we bring?' I asked.

'Gooseberry jam.'

'Just the thing. Empty the bottle!'

The dish was a great success. Everyone enjoyed it, including Mr Oliver, who had no idea what went into it.

'What's this called?' he asked.

'It's an all-Indian sweet-and-sour jam-potato curry,' I ventured.

'For short, just call it a Bond-bhujji,' said Bimal.

I had earned my cookery badge!

*

Poor Mr Oliver! He wasn't really cut out to be a Scoutmaster, any more than I was meant to be a Scout. The following day he announced that he would give us a lesson in tracking. He would take a half-hour start and walk into the forest, leaving behind him a trail of broken twigs, chicken feathers, pine cones and chestnuts, and we were to follow the trail until we found him.

Unfortunately, we were not very good trackers. We did follow Mr Oliver's trail some way into the forest, but were distracted by a pool of clear water which looked very inviting. Abandoning our uniforms, we jumped into the pool and had a great time romping around or just lying on the grassy banks and enjoying the sunshine. A couple of hours later, feeling hungry, we returned to our campsite and set about preparing the evening meal. Bond-bhujji again, but with further variations.

It was growing dark, and we were beginning to worry about Mr Oliver's whereabouts when he limped into camp, assisted by a couple of local villagers. Having waited for us at the far end of the forest for a couple of hours, he had decided to come back by following his own trail, but in the gathering gloom he was soon lost. Some locals returning from the temple took charge of him and escorted him back to camp. He was very angry and made us return all our good-conduct and other badges, which he stuffed into his haversack. I had to give up my cookery badge too.

An hour later, when we were all preparing to get into our sleeping bags for the night, Mr Oliver called out: 'Where's dinner?'

'We've had ours,' said Bimal. 'Everything is finished, sir.'

'Where's Bond? He's supposed to be the cook. Bond, get up and make me an omelette.'

'Can't, sir.'

'Why not?'

'You have my badge. Not allowed to cook without it. Scout rule, sir.'

'Never heard of such a rule. But you can have your badges back, all of you. We return to school tomorrow.'

Mr Oliver returned to his tent in a huff. But I relented and made him an elaborate omelette, garnishing it with dandelion leaves and an extra chilli.

'Never had such an omelette before,' confessed Mr Oliver, blowing out his cheeks. 'A little too hot, but otherwise quite interesting.'

'Would you like another, sir?'

'Tomorrow, Bond, tomorrow. We'll breakfast early tomorrow.'

But we had to break up our camp very early the next day. In the early hours, a bear had strayed into our camp, entered the tent where our stores were kept, and created havoc with all our provisions, even rolling our biggest *degchi* down the hillside.

In the confusion and uproar that followed, the bear entered Mr Oliver's tent (he was already outside, fortunately) and came out entangled in Mr Oliver's dressing gown. It then made off in the direction of the forest.

A bear in a dressing gown? It was a comical sight. And though we were a troop of brave little Scouts, we thought it better to let the bear keep the gown.

The Big Race

I was awakened by the sound of a hornbill honking in the banyan tree. I lay in bed, looking through the open window as the early morning sunshine crept up the wall. I knew it was a holiday, and that there was something important to be done that day, but for some time I couldn't quite remember what it was. Then, as the room got brighter, and the hornbill stopped his noise, I remembered.

It was the day of the big race.

I leapt out of bed, pulled open a dressing table drawer and brought out a cardboard box punctured with little holes. I opened the lid to see if Maharani was all right.

Maharani, my bamboo-beetle, was asleep on the core of an apple. I had given her a week's rigorous training for the monsoon beetle race, and she was enjoying a well-earned rest before the big event. I did not disturb her.

Closing the box, I crept out of the house by the back door. I did not want my parents to see me sneaking off to the municipal park at that early hour.

When I reached the gardens, the early morning sun was just beginning to make emeralds of the dewdrops, and the grass was cool and springy to my bare feet. A group of boys had gathered in a corner of the gardens, and among them were Kamal and Anil.

Anil's black rhino beetle was the favourite. It was a big beetle, with an aggressive forehead rather like its owner's. It was called Black Prince. Kamal's beetle was quite ordinary in size, but it possessed a long pair of whiskers (I suspected it belonged to the cockroach rather than the beetle family), and was called Moochha, which is Hindi for moustache.

There were one or two other entries, but none of them looked promising, and interest centred on Black Prince, Moochha, and my own Maharani who was still asleep on her apple core. A few bets were being made, in coins or marbles, and a prize for the winner was on display: a great stag beetle, quite dangerous to look at, which would enable the winner to start a stable and breed beetles on a large scale.

There was some confusion when Kamal's Moochha escaped from his box and took a preliminary canter over the grass, but he was soon caught and returned to his paddock. Moochha appeared to be in good form, and several boys put their marbles on him.

The course was about six feet long, the tracks six inches wide. The tracks were fenced with strips of cardboard so that the contestants would not move over to each other's path or leave the course altogether. They could only go forwards or backwards. They were held at the starting point by another piece of cardboard, which would be placed behind them as soon as the race began.

A little Sikh boy in a yellow pyjama suit was acting as starter, and he kept blowing his whistle for order and attention. Eventually he gained enough silence in which to announce the rules of the race: the contesting beetles were not allowed to be touched during the race, or blown at from behind, or bribed forward with bits of food. Only moral assistance was allowed, in the form of cheering and advice.

Moochha and Black Prince were already at the starting point, but Maharani seemed unwilling to leave her apple core, and I had to drag her to the starting post. There was further delay when Moochha got his whiskers entangled in the legs of a rival, but they were soon separated and the beetles placed in separate lanes. The race was about to start.

Kamal sat on his haunches, very quiet and serious, looking from Moochha to the finishing line and back again. I was biting my nails. Anil's bushy eyebrows were bunched together in a scowl. There was a tense hush amongst the spectators.

'Pee-ee-eep!' went the whistle.

And they were off!

Or rather, Moochha and Black Prince were off because Maharani was still at the starting post, wondering what had happened to her apple core.

Everyone was cheering madly, Anil was jumping about, and Kamal was shouting himself hoarse.

Moochha was going at a spanking rate. Black Prince really wasn't taking much interest in the proceedings, but at least he was moving, and everything could happen in a race of this nature. I was furious. All the coaching I had given Maharani appeared to be of no use. She was still looking confused and a little resentful at having been deprived of her apple.

Then Moochha suddenly stopped, about two feet from the finish line. He seemed to be having trouble with his whiskers, and kept twitching them this way and that. Black Prince was catching up inch by inch, and both Anil and Kamal were hopping about with excitement. Nobody was paying any attention to Maharani, who was looking suspiciously at the other beetles in the rear. No doubt she suspected them of having something to do with the disappearance of her apple. I begged her to make an effort. It was with difficulty that I prevented myself from giving her a push, as that would have meant disqualification.

As Black Prince drew level with Moochha, he stopped and appeared to be enquiring about his rival's whiskers. Anil and Kamal now became even more frantic in their efforts to encourage their racers, and the cheering on all sides was deafening.

Maharani, enraged at having been deprived of her apple core, now decided to make a bid for liberty and rushed forward in great style.

I gave a cry of joy, but the others did not notice this new challenge until Maharani had drawn level with her rivals. There was a gasp of surprise from the spectators, and Maharani dashed across the finish line in record time.

Everyone cheered the gallant outsider. Anil and Kamal very sportingly shook my hand and congratulated me on my methods. Coins and marbles

passed from hand to hand. The little Sikh boy blew his whistle for silence and presented me with the first prize.

I examined the new beetle with respect and gently stroked its hard, smooth back. Then, in case Maharani should feel jealous, I put away the prize beetle and returned Maharani to her apple core. I was determined that I would not indulge in any favouritism.

A Plea for Bowlers

Cricket never will be fair
Till bowlers get their rightful share
For toiling in the midday sun.
What should be done?
It's simple —
Make those wickets broader, taller!
That should make it much more fun
For the poor perspiring bowler.
P.S. And in the interest of the game
The size of the bat remains the same.

Four Boys on a Glacier

[Excerpt from *The Hidden Pool*, an adventure story about three friends, Laurie, Kamal and Anil, who decide to trek up the Pindari Glacier as a culmination to their school holidays.]

To the Hills

At the end of August, when the rains were nearly over, we met at the pool to make plans for the autumn holidays. We had bathed and were stretched out in the shade of the fresh, rain-washed sal trees, when Kamal, pointing vaguely to the distant mountains, said: 'Why don't we go to the Pindari Glacier?'

'The glacier!' exclaimed Anil. 'But that's all snow and ice!'

'Of course it is,' said Kamal. 'But there's a path through the mountains that goes all the way to the foot of the glacier. It's only fifty-four miles.'

'Only fifty-four miles! Do you mean we must— *walk* fifty-four miles?'

'Well, there's no other way,' said Kamal. 'Unless you prefer to sit on a mule. But your legs are too long, they'll be trailing along the ground. No, we'll have to walk. It will take us about ten days to get to the glacier and back, but if we take enough food there'll be no problem. There are dak bungalows to stay in at night.'

'Kamal gets all the best ideas,' I said. 'But I suppose Anil and I will have to get our parents' permission. And some money.'

'My mother won't let me go,' said Anil. 'She says the mountains are full of ghosts. And she thinks I'll get up to some mischief. How can one get up to mischief on a lonely mountain? Have you been on the mountains, Laurie?'

'I've been on English mountains,' I said, 'but they're not half as high as these. Kamal seems to know about them.'

'Only what I've read in books,' said Kamal. 'I'm sure it won't be dangerous, people are always going to the glacier. Can you see that peak above the others on the right?' He pointed to the distant snow range, barely visible against the soft blue sky. 'The Pindari Glacier is below it. It's at 12,000 feet, I think, but we won't need any special equipment. There'll be snow only for the final two or three miles. Do you know that it's the beginning of the river Sarayu?'

'You mean our river?' asked Anil, thinking of the little river that wandered along the outskirts of the town, joining the Ganges further downstream.

'Yes. But it's only a trickle where it starts.'

'How much money will we need?' I asked, determined to be practical.

'Well, I've saved twenty rupees,' said Kamal.

'But won't you need that for your books?' I asked.

'No, this is extra. If each of us brings twenty rupees, we should have enough. There's nothing to spend money on, once we are up on the mountains. There are only one or two villages on the way and food is scarce, so we'll have to take plenty of food with us. I learnt all this from the tourist office.'

'Kamal's been planning this without our knowledge,' complained Anil.

'He always plans in advance,' I said. 'But it's a good idea, and it should be a fine adventure.'

'All right,' said Anil. 'But Laurie will have to be with me when I ask my mother. She thinks Laurie is very sensible, and might let me go if he says it's quite safe.' And he ended the discussion by jumping into the pool, where we soon joined him.

Though my mother hesitated about letting me go, my father said it was a wonderful idea and was only sorry because he couldn't accompany us himself (which was a relief, as we didn't want our parents along); and though Anil's father hesitated—or rather, because he hesitated—his mother said yes, of course Anil must go, the mountain air would be good for his health. A puzzling remark, because Anil's health had never been better. The bazaar people, when they heard that Anil might be away for a couple of weeks, were overjoyed at the prospect of a quiet spell, and pressed his father to let him go.

On a cloudy day, promising rain, we bundled ourselves into the bus that was to take us to Kapkote (where people lose their caps and coats, punned Anil), the starting point of our trek. Each of us carried a haversack, and we had also brought along a good-sized bedding roll which, apart from blankets, also contained rice and flour thoughtfully provided by Anil's mother. We had no idea how we would carry the bedding roll once we started walking. But we didn't worry much over minor details: an astrologer had told Anil's mother it was a good day for travelling, so we decided all would be well.

We were soon in the hills, on a winding road that took us up and up, until we saw the valley and our town spread out beneath us, the river a silver ribbon across the plain. Kamal pointed to a patch of dense sal forest and said, 'Our pool must be there!' We took a sharp bend, and the valley disappeared, and the mountains towered above us.

We had dull headaches by the time we reached Kapkote, but when we got down from the bus a cool breeze freshened us. At the wayside shop we drank glasses of hot, sweet tea, and the shopkeeper told us we could spend the night in one of his rooms. It was pleasant at Kapkote, the hills wooded with deodar trees, the lower slopes planted with fresh green paddy. At night, there was a wind moaning in the trees and it found its way through the cracks in the windows and eventually through our blankets. Then, right outside the door, a dog began howling at the moon. It had been a good day for travelling, but the astrologer hadn't warned us that it would be a bad night for sleep.

Next morning, we washed our faces at a small stream about a hundred yards from the shop and filled our water bottles for the day's march. A boy from the nearby village sat on a rock, studying our movements.

'Where are you going?' he asked, unable to suppress his curiosity.

'To the glacier,' said Kamal.

'Let me come with you,' said the boy. 'I know the way.'

'You're too small,' said Anil. 'We need someone who can carry our bedding roll.'

'I'm small,' said the boy, 'but I'm strong. I'm not a weakling like the boys in the plains.' Though he was shorter than any of us, he certainly looked sturdy, and had a muscular well-knit body and pink cheeks. 'See!' he said, and picking up a rock the size of a football, he heaved it across the stream.

'I think he can come with us,' I said.

And the boy, whose name was Bisnu, dashed off to inform his people of his employment—we had agreed to pay him a rupee a day for acting as tour guide and Sherpa.

And then we started walking, at first, above the little Sarayu river, then climbing higher along the rough mule track, always within sound of the water.

Kamal wanted to bathe in the river. I said it was too far, and Anil said we wouldn't reach the dak bungalow before dark if we went for a swim.

Regretfully, we left the river behind, and marched on through a forest of oaks, over wet, rotting leaves that made a soft carpet for our feet. We ate at noon, under an oak. As we didn't want to waste any time making a fire—not on this first crucial day—we ate beans from a tin and drank most of our water.

In the afternoon we came to the river again. The water was swifter now, green and bubbling still far below us. We saw two boys in the water, swimming in an inlet which reminded us of our own secret pool. They waved, and invited us to join them. We returned their greeting but it would have taken us an hour to get down to the river and up again; so we continued on our way.

We walked fifteen miles on that first day—our speed was to decrease after this and we were at the dak bungalow by six o'clock. Bisnu busied himself collecting sticks for a fire. Anil found the bungalow's watchman asleep in a patch of fading sunlight and roused him.

The watchman, who hadn't come by visitors for weeks, grumbled at our intrusion, but opened a room for us. He also produced some potatoes from his quarters, and these we roasted for dinner.

It became cold after the sun had gone down and we remained close to Bisnu's fire. The damp sticks burnt fitfully. By this time Bisnu had fully justified his inclusion in our party. He had balanced the bedding roll on his shoulders as though it were full of cotton wool instead of blankets. Now he was helping with the cooking. And we were glad to have him sharing our hot potatoes and strong tea.

There were only two beds in the room and we pushed these together, apportioning out the blankets as fairly as possible. Then the four of us leapt into bed, shivering in the cold. We were already over 5000 feet. Bisnu, in his own peculiar way, had wrapped a scarf round his neck, though a cotton singlet and shorts were all that he wore for the night.

'Tell us a story, Laurie,' said Anil. 'It will help us to fall asleep.'

I told them one of his mother's stories, about a boy and a girl who had been changed into a pair of buffaloes, and then Bisnu told us about the ghost of a sadhu, who was to be seen sitting in the snow by moonlight not far from the glacier. Far from putting us to sleep, this story kept us awake for hours.

'Aren't you asleep yet?' I asked Anil in the middle of the night.

'No, you keep kicking me,' he lied.

'We don't have enough blankets,' complained Kamal. 'It's too cold to sleep.'

'I never sleep till it's very late,' mumbled Bisnu from the bottom of the bed.

No one was prepared to admit that our imaginations were keeping us awake.

After a little while we heard a thud on the corrugated tin sheets, and then the sound of someone—or something—scrambling about on the roof. Anil, Kamal and I sat up in bed, startled out of our wits. Bisnu, who had won the race to be the first one to fall asleep, merely turned over on his side and grunted.

'It's only a bear,' he said. 'Didn't you notice the pumpkins on the roof? Bears love pumpkins.'

For half an hour we had to listen to the bear as it clambered about on the roof, feasting on the watchman's ripening pumpkins. Finally, there was silence. Kamal and I crawled out of our blankets and went to the window. And through the frosted glass we saw a black Himalayan bear ambling across the slope in front of the bungalow, a fat pumpkin held between its paws.

To the River

It was raining when we woke up and the mountains were obscured by a heavy mist. We delayed our departure, playing football on the veranda with one of the pumpkins that had fallen off the roof. At noon the rain stopped and the sun shone through the clouds. As the mist lifted, we saw the snow range, the great peaks of Nanda Kot and Trishul stepping into the sky.

'It's different up here,' said Kamal. 'I feel a different person.'

'That's the altitude,' I said. 'As we go higher, we'll get lighter in the head.'

'Anil is light in the head already,' said Kamal. 'I hope the altitude isn't too much for him.'

'If you two are going to be witty,' said Anil, 'I shall go off with Bisnu, and you'll have to find the way yourselves.'

Bisnu grinned at each of us in turn to show us that he wasn't taking sides, and after a breakfast of boiled eggs, we set off on our trek to the next bungalow.

Rain had made the ground slippery and we were soon ankle-deep in slush. Our next bungalow lay in a narrow valley, on the banks of the rushing Pindar river, which twisted its way through the mountains. We were not sure how far we had to go, but nobody seemed to be in a hurry. On an impulse, I decided to hurry on ahead of the others.

I wanted to be waiting for them at the river.

The path dropped steeply, then rose and went round a big mountain. I met a woodcutter and asked him how far it was to the river. He was a short, stocky man, with gnarled hands and a weathered face.

'Seven miles,' he said. 'Are you alone?'

'No, the others are following but I cannot wait for them. If you meet them, tell them I'll be waiting at the river.'

The path descended steeply now, and I had to run a little. It was a dizzy, winding path. The hillside was covered with lush green ferns and, in the trees, unseen birds sang loudly. Soon I was in the valley and the path straightened out.

A girl was coming from the opposite direction.

She held a long, curved knife, with which she had been cutting grass and fodder. There were rings in her nose and ears and her arms were covered with heavy bangles. The bangles made music when she moved her hands: it was as though her hands spoke a language of their own.

'How far is it to the river?' I asked.

The girl had probably never been near the river, or she may have been thinking of another one, because she replied, 'Twenty miles,' without any hesitation.

I laughed and ran down the path. A parrot screeched suddenly, flew low over my head—a flash of blue and green—and took the course of the path, while I followed its dipping flight, until the path rose and the bird disappeared into the trees.

A trickle of water came from the hillside and I stopped to drink. The water was cold and sharp and very refreshing. I had walked alone for nearly an hour. Presently, I saw a boy ahead of me, driving a few goats along the path.

'How far is it to the river?' I asked, when I caught up with him.

The boy said, 'Oh, not far, just round the next hill.'

As I was hungry, I produced some dry bread from my pocket and, breaking it in two, offered half to the boy. We sat on the grassy hillside and ate in silence. Then we walked on together and began talking; and talking, I did not notice the smarting of my feet and the distance I had covered.

But after some time the boy had to diverge along another path, and I was once more on my own.

I missed the village boy. I looked up and down the path, but I could see no one, no sign of Anil and Kamal and Bisnu, and the river was not in sight either. I began to feel discouraged. But I couldn't turn back; I was determined to be at the river before the others.

And so I walked on, along the muddy path, past terraced fields and small stone houses, until there were no more fields and houses, only forest and sun and silence.

The silence was impressive and a little frightening.

It was different from the silence of a room or an empty street. Nor was there any movement, except for the bending of grass beneath my feet and the circling of a hawk high above the fir trees.

And then, as I rounded a sharp bend, the silence broke into sound.

The sound of the river.

Far down in the valley, the river tumbled over itself in its impatience to reach the plains. I began to run, slipped and stumbled, but continued running.

And the water was blue and white and wonderful.

When Anil, Kamal and Bisnu arrived, the four of us bravely decided to bathe in the little river. The late afternoon sun was still warm, but the water—so clear and inviting—proved to be ice-cold. Only twenty miles upstream the river emerged as a little trickle from the glacier and, in its swift descent down the mountain slopes, did not give the sun a chance to penetrate its waters. But we were determined to bathe, to wash away the dust and sweat of our two days' trudging, and we leapt about in the shallows like startled porpoises, slapping water on each other and gasping with the shock of each immersion.

Bisnu, more accustomed to mountain streams than ourselves, ventured across in an attempt to catch an otter, but wasn't fast enough. Then we were on the springy grass, wrestling each other in order to get warm.

The bungalow stood on a ledge just above the river, and the sound of the water rushing down the mountain slope could be heard at all times. The sound of the birds, which we had grown used to, was drowned by the sound of the water, but the birds themselves could be seen, many-coloured, standing out splendidly against the dark green forest foliage: the red-crowned jay, the paradise flycatcher, the purple whistling thrush and others that we could not recognize.

Higher up the mountain, above some terraced land where oats and barley were grown, stood a small cluster of huts. This, we were told by the watchman, was the last village on the way to the glacier. It was, in fact, one of the last villages in India, because if we crossed the difficult passes beyond the glacier, we would find ourselves in Tibet.

We told the watchman we would be quite satisfied if we reached the glacier.

Then Anil made the mistake of mentioning the Abominable Snowman, of whom we had been reading in the papers. The people of Nepal believe in the existence of the Snowman, and our watchman was a Nepali.

'Yes, I have seen the Yeti,' he told us. 'A great shaggy flat-footed creature. In winter, when it snows heavily, he passes by the bungalow at night. I have seen his tracks the next morning.'

'Does he come this way in summer?' I asked anxiously. We were sitting before another of Bisnu's fires, drinking tea with condensed milk, and trying to get through a black, sticky sweet which the watchman had produced from his tin trunk.

'The Yeti doesn't come here in summer,' said the old man. 'But I have seen the Lidini sometimes. You have to be careful of her.'

'What is a Lidini?' asked Kamal.

'Ah!' said the watchman mysteriously. 'You have heard of the Abominable Snowman, no doubt, but there are few who have heard of the Abominable Snow woman! And yet, she is far more dangerous of the two!'

'What is she like?' asked Anil, and we all craned forward.

'She is of the same height as the Yeti—about seven feet when her back is straight—and her hair is much longer. She has very long teeth and nails. Her feet face inwards, but she can run very fast, especially downhill. If you see a Lidini and she chases you, always run uphill. She tires quickly because of her feet. But when running down hills she has no trouble at all, and you have to be very fast to escape her!'

'Well, we're all good runners,' said Anil with a nervous laugh. 'But it's just a fairy story, I don't believe a word of it.'

'But you *must* believe fairy stories,' I said, remembering a performance of *Peter Pan* in London, when those in the audience who believed in fairies were asked to clap their hands in order to save Tinker

139

Bell's life. 'Even if they aren't true,' I added, deciding there was a world of difference between Tinker Bell and the Abominable Snow woman.

'Well, I don't believe there's a Snowman or a Snow woman!' declared Anil.

The watchman was most offended and refused to tell us anything about the Sagpa and Sagpani; but Bisnu knew about them, and later, when we were in bed, he told us that they were similar to Snowmen but much smaller. Their favourite pastime was to sleep, and they became very annoyed if anyone woke them up, and became ferocious, and did not give one much time to start running uphill.

The Sagpa and Sagpani sometimes kidnapped small children and, taking them to their cave, would look after the children very carefully, feeding them on fruit, honey, rice, and earthworms.

'When the Sagpa isn't looking,' he said, 'you can throw the earthworms over your shoulder.'

Trek up the Glacier

It was a fine sunny morning when we set out to cover the last seven miles to the glacier. We had expected this to be a stiff climb, but the last dak bungalow was situated at well over 10,000 feet above sea level, and the ascent was to be fairly gradual.

And then suddenly, abruptly, there were no more trees. As the bungalow dropped out of sight, the trees and bushes gave way to short grass and little blue and pink alpine flowers. The snow peaks were close now, ringing us in on every side. We passed waterfalls, cascading hundreds of feet down precipitous rock faces, thundering into the little river. A great golden eagle hovered over us for some time.

'I feel different again,' said Kamal.

'We're very high now,' I said. 'I hope we won't get headaches.'

'I've got one already,' complained Anil. 'Let's have some tea.'

We had left our cooking utensils at the bungalow, expecting to return there for the night, and had brought with us only a few biscuits, chocolate, and a thermos of tea. We finished the tea, and Bisnu scrambled about on the grassy slopes, collecting wild strawberries. They were tiny strawberries, very sweet, and they did nothing to satisfy our appetites. There was no sign of habitation or human life. The only creatures to be found at that height were the gurals—sure-footed mountain goats—and an occasional snow leopard or bear.

We found and explored a small cave and then, turning a bend, came unexpectedly upon the glacier.

The hill fell away and there, confronting us, was a great white field of snow and ice, cradled between two peaks that could only have been the abode of the gods. We were speechless for several minutes. Kamal took my hand and held on to it for reassurance; perhaps he was not sure that what he saw was real. Anil's mouth hung open. Bisnu's eyes glittered with excitement.

We proceeded cautiously on the snow, supporting each other on the slippery surface, but we could not go far, because we were quite unequipped for any high-altitude climbing. It was pleasant to feel that we were the only boys in our town who had climbed so high. A few black rocks jutted out from the snow, and we sat down on them to feast our eyes on the view. The sun reflected sharply from the snow and we felt surprisingly warm.

'Let's sunbathe!' said Anil, on a sudden impulse.

'Yes, let's do that!' I said.

In a few minutes we had taken off our clothes and, sitting on the rocks, were exposing ourselves to the elements. It was delicious to feel the sun crawling over my skin. Within half an hour I was a postbox red, and so was Bisnu, and the two of us decided to get into our clothes before the sun scorched the skin off our backs. Kamal and Anil appeared to be more resilient to sunlight and laughed at our discomfiture. Bisnu and I avenged ourselves by gathering up handfuls of snow and rubbing it on their backs. They dressed quickly enough after that, Anil leaping about like a performing monkey.

Meanwhile, almost imperceptibly, clouds had covered some of the peaks, and a white mist drifted down the mountain slopes. It was time to get back to the bungalow; we would barely make it before dark.

We had not gone far when lightning began to sizzle above the mountaintops, followed by waves of thunder.

'Let's run!' shouted Anil, 'We can take shelter in the cave!'

The clouds could hold themselves in no longer, and the rain came down suddenly, stinging our faces as it was whipped up by an icy wind. Half-blinded, we ran as fast as we could along the slippery path and stumbled, drenched and exhausted, into the little cave.

The cave was mercifully dry and not very dark. We remained at the entrance, watching the rain sweep past us, listening to the wind whistling down the long gorge.

'It will take some time to stop,' said Kamal.

'No, it will pass soon,' said Bisnu. 'These storms are short and fierce.'

Anil produced his pocket knife and, to pass the time, we carved our names in the smooth rock of the cave.

'We will come here again, when we are older,' said Kamal, 'and perhaps our names will still be here.'

It had grown dark by the time the rain stopped. A full moon helped us find our way. We went slowly and carefully. The rain had loosened the earth and stones kept rolling down the hillside. I was afraid of starting a landslide.

'I hope we don't meet the Lidini now,' said Anil fervently.

'I thought you didn't believe in her,' I said.

'I don't,' replied Anil. 'But what if I'm wrong?'

We saw only a gural, poised on the brow of a precipice, silhouetted against the sky.

And then the path vanished.

Had it not been for the bright moonlight, we might have walked straight into an empty void. The rain had caused a landslide and where there had been a narrow path there was now only a precipice of loose, slippery shale.

'We'll have to go back,' said Bisnu. 'It will be too dangerous to try and cross in the dark.'

'We'll sleep in the cave,' I suggested.

'We've nothing to sleep in,' said Anil. 'Not a single blanket between us — and nothing to eat!'

'We just have to rough it till morning,' said Kamal. 'It will be better than breaking our necks here.'

We returned to the cave, which did at least have the virtue of being dry. Bisnu had matches and he made a fire with some dry sticks which had been left in the cave by a previous party. We ate what was left of a loaf of bread.

There was no sleep for any of us that night. We lay close to each other for comfort, but the ground was hard and uneven. And every noise we heard outside the cave made us think of leopards and bears and even Abominable Snowmen.

We got up as soon as there was a faint glow in the sky. The snow peaks were bright pink, but we were too tired and hungry and worried to care for the beauty of the sunrise. We took the path to the landslide and once again looked for a way across. Kamal ventured to take a few steps on the loose pebbles, but the ground gave way immediately, and we had to grab him by the arms and shoulders to prevent him from sliding a hundred feet down the gorge.

'Now what are we going to do?' I asked.

'Look for another way,' said Bisnu.

'But do you know of any?'

And we all turned to look at Bisnu, expecting him to provide the solution to our problems.

'I have heard of a way,' said Bisnu, 'but I have never used it. It will be a little dangerous, I think. The path has not been used for several years — not since the traders stopped coming in from Tibet.'

'Never mind, we'll try it,' said Anil.

'We will have to cross the glacier first,' said Bisnu. 'That's the main problem.'

We looked at each other in silence. The glacier didn't look difficult to cross, but we knew that it would not be easy for novices like us. For almost a quarter of a mile it consisted of hard, slippery ice.

Anil was the first to arrive at a decision.

'Come on,' he said. 'There's no time to waste.'

We were soon on the glacier. And we remained on it for a long time. For every two steps forward, we slid one step backward. Our progress was slow and awkward. Sometimes, after advancing several yards across the ice at a steep incline, one of us would slip back and the others would have to slither down to help him up. At one particularly difficult spot, I dropped our water bottle and, grabbing at it, lost my footing, fell full-length and went sliding some twenty feet down the icy slope.

I had sprained my wrist and hurt my knee, and was to prove a liability for the rest of the trek.

Kamal tied his handkerchief round my hand, and Anil took charge of the water bottle, which we had filled with ice. Using my good hand to grab Bisnu's legs whenever I slipped, I struggled on behind the others.

It was almost noon, and we were quite famished, when we put our feet on grass again. And then we had another steep climb, clutching at roots and grasses, before we reached the path that Bisnu had spoken about. It was little more than a goat track, but it took us round the mountain and brought us within sight of the dak bungalow.

'I could eat a whole chicken,' said Kamal.

I could eat two,' I said.

'I could eat a Snowman,' said Bisnu.

'And I could eat the chowkidar,' said Anil.

Fortunately for the chowkidar, he had anticipated our hunger, and when we staggered into the bungalow

late in the afternoon, we found a meal waiting for us. True, there was no chicken, but so ravenous did we feel, that even the lowly onion tasted delicious!

We had Bisnu to thank for getting us back successfully. He had brought us over mountain and glacier with all the skill and confidence of a boy who had the Himalayas in his blood.

Reed more in Puffin

Uncles, Aunts and Elephants: Tales from your Favourite Storyteller
by Ruskin Bond

A timeless selection of writings from India's best-loved author

I know the world's a crowded place,
And elephants do take up space,
But if it makes a difference, Lord,
I'd gladly share my room and board.
A baby elephant would do…
But, if he brings his mother too,
There's Dad's garage. He wouldn't mind.
To elephants, he's more than kind.
But I wonder what my Mum would say
If their aunts and uncles came to stay!

Ruskin Bond has regaled generations of readers for decades. This delightful collection of poetry, prose and non-fiction brings together some of his best work in a single volume. Sumptuously illustrated, *Uncles, Aunts and Elephants : Tales From Your Favourite Storyteller* is a book to treasure for all times.

Coming Soon in Puffin

Rusty and the Magic Mountain
by Ruskin Bond

If you go looking for adventure, you will find it

Rusty and his friends Pitambar and Popat find adventure in no small measure when they set out to climb a mysterious mountain around which legend and superstition has grown over the years. On the way they shelter in a haunted rest house, encounter a tiger, and experience a hilarious mule ride which takes them to the palace of a mad Rani who presides over a murder of crows. There are other surprises in store for the boys—a beautiful but mysterious princess, a colony of dwarfs and a wonderful musical stone!

Veteran author Ruskin Bond returns with a brand new Rusty adventure after more than a decade. A rollicking tale of humour and enchantment, *Rusty and the Magic Mountain* will win the much-loved character of Rusty a whole new band of followers.